TEA IS FOR TRAPPED

A HAUNTED TEAROOM COZY MYSTERY

KAREN SUE WALKER

LARAGRAY PRESS

Published by Laragray Press

This is a work of fiction. All names, characters, locales, and incidents are products of the author's imagination and any resemblance to actual people, places, or events is coincidental.

Note from the Publisher: The recipes contained in this book have been tested, and to our knowledge are correct if followed exactly as written. Cooking and baking are subject to variables outside of our control; we are not responsible for results due to errors or typos in the ingredients or instructions. The publisher and author are not responsible for any adverse reactions to the recipes contained in this book.

TO MY READERS

Thank you for joining April May on her journey through ten Haunted Tearoom cozy mysteries. When I first wrote about her getting two flat tires in Serenity Cove, I never imagined I'd one day be wrapping up book ten!

It's all because of you.

You read the books, shared them with friends, left reviews, and sent me encouraging emails, so I kept writing about April May, Jennifer, Irma, and all the other residents of Serenity Cove (and the ghosts, of course!)

You're the reason these stories came to life, and I'm so grateful to have you along for the ride.

ACKNOWLEDGMENTS

My gorgeous cover was designed by Mariah Sinclair, the Cozy Cover Queen. You can find her at mariahsinclairdesign.com.

As always, special thanks to my beta readers, typo catchers, and early reviewers—I'm so grateful to you for your support!

Sign up for email updates at karensuewalker.com and I'll do my best to keep your inbox full of everything cozy.

CHAPTER 1

The heavenly aroma of shortbread filled my Victorian kitchen as I pulled a sheet of cookies from the oven and transferred them to a wire rack. Outside, the morning fog hung low over the ocean, but inside, we were warm and cozy as we prepared for the day's event, a Sherlock Holmes-themed tea. I was grateful to have Jennifer, my assistant, along with my friend and neighbor, Irma, helping me assemble tiered trays of scones, finger sandwiches, and desserts.

Irma took a break from peeling hard-boiled eggs to take a few sips of her freshly frothed mocha. The door to the kitchen swung open, and Jennifer entered wearing a nineteenth-century servant's uniform complete with starched apron. Her outfit was quite a contrast to Irma's Led Zeppelin tee and cargo pants.

I stopped stacking cookies to give her costume the attention it deserved. "You look like you just stepped right out of a historical novel."

"Like one of those bodice rippers with Fabio on the cover?" Irma asked. "You must be the naughty servant girl."

Jennifer pretended she hadn't heard as she waved a pair of lace-trimmed napkins. "We don't have enough vintage linens."

"I doubt anybody is going to care if the napkins match," Irma said bluntly. "Anyway, Sherlock Holmes probably used his sleeve."

Jennifer raised an eyebrow. "I think he'd at least use his handkerchief."

I stepped between them with my spatula held like a sword. "Let's use the black ones from the holiday box. No one needs to know they're our Halloween napkins."

Jennifer grabbed the keys to the garage where we kept extra supplies. She dashed off, her ponytail bouncing behind her like a perky exclamation point. At twenty-six, Jennifer had a zest for life that sometimes made me feel ancient.

By now, Irma had progressed to chopping the eggs. "You really think this group is gonna show up dressed like Sherlock Holmes and company?"

"I hope so, or Jennifer will be very disappointed. According to the Holmes Society of Northern California website, they take their cosplay seriously." I tapped my phone, already pulled up to the group's homepage.

Irma stared at the screen. "Is that man wearing a deerstalker hat or a dead squirrel?"

"That's Greg Timmons, Esquire. A retired lawyer, apparently." I pinched out to zoom on a photo of a distinguished-looking gentleman in full Sherlock costume, complete with magnifying glass and an expression of such pompous self-satisfaction that I nearly laughed out loud. "He's the vice president of the society. The woman next to him is the president, Delilah Smith." I squinted at the small print. "She's dressed as Irene Adler. Apparently, Sherlock Holmes referred to her as 'The Woman.'"

"As if there were only one?"

"Right?" I scrolled to another picture of a couple dressed as Dr. John and Mrs. Mary Watson. The woman, whose real name was Rosalie Kent according to the caption, had a round face and a gentle smile, while the man, Todd McGrady, seemed to fade into the background despite his dapper costume. "Should be an interesting afternoon."

Irma added globs of mayonnaise, mustard, and several other ingredients to the chopped eggs, including pickle juice and a dash of cayenne pepper. "What kind of wackadoodles dress up like people who aren't even real?"

"Don't you dare say that in front of Jennifer." I set a thinly sliced loaf of bakery-fresh white bread on the kitchen island. "Lots of people have hobbies. Like me. People used to tease me about throwing tea parties, but now that it's my business, no one says a thing."

"You have other interests," Irma said. "Although I'm not sure I'd call hanging out with ghosts a hobby."

I lowered my voice as if some stray spirit might hear me. "Now that you mention it, I haven't seen a ghost in weeks."

That got Irma's attention. She'd known about my unwanted ability to see the deceased since shortly after I moved to town. Unlike the way most people would have reacted, Irma had simply nodded and said, "That explains the weird conversations I've overheard you having with yourself."

"It's kinda nice when I'm alone in the kitchen to actually be *alone* in the kitchen."

"Hmmm..." Irma leaned closer. "But have you heard any bumps in the night or felt chills or creepy vibes?" Irma might pretend to be unflappable, but ghost stories were her guilty pleasure.

"Not a peep, not a cold spot, not even a gust of cold wind. Pearl loved New Orleans so much, I think she convinced George to stay there with her. Forever, I hope." I almost missed Pearl with her 1920s slang, her flapper dresses, and the way she butchered the English language, but I definitely didn't miss her grating voice.

The deep creases around Irma's eyes, earned from seven decades of skeptical squinting, deepened further. "Are you sure you're ghost-free? They followed you cross-country before."

"This time it's different," I said, in the same tone people use to justify getting back together with their ex. "I think they've finally found a haunt that suits them." I began buttering bread slices, passing them two at a time to Irma to assemble the egg salad sandwiches. I'd learned that a thin layer of butter kept the bread from getting soggy.

Jennifer returned with the napkins. "Found them! I'll run them through a quick rinse cycle to freshen them up." She shook one over the trash and something orange and sparkling flittered out of the folds. "After I get rid of the orange sparkles that stuck to them from the Halloween decorations."

"I'm going to take one more look at the room, just to make sure everything looks perfect." I didn't wait around for Jennifer or Irma to tell me I'd already checked several times.

Entering the study, I felt my shoulders relax. With Jennifer's help, I'd completely redecorated the room to resemble a cozy English library in an old manor house, with heavy velvet drapes and oil paintings of landscapes and hunting scenes. Dark mahogany bookshelves lined the walls, filled with leather-bound books I'd collected over the years. Velvet-upholstered chairs had been pushed aside to make room for a dozen round tables covered in forest green tablecloths.

The chime of the doorbell signaled the arrival of our cosplaying group. I reassured myself that we'd thought of everything and left the study to greet our first guests of the day. Through the etched glass of the front door, I caught a glimpse of a clean-shaven man wearing a deerstalker hat and two women in period dresses.

I took a deep breath. "It's showtime."

CHAPTER 2

I hurried to answer the door and held it open wide to give the three guests and their costumes room to enter. "Welcome. I'm April May, the proprietress of SereniTea Tearoom."

The man, who I recognized from the website photos, barely managed to say hello before the older of the two women pushed past him. She was dressed in a plain, brown costume with huge sleeves, a high, lace-trimmed collar, and a hat trimmed with what appeared to be a bouquet of small pheasants. Her bright red lipstick stood in stark contrast to her severe expression, and the brooch pinned to her high collar, clearly an expensive antique, sparkled in the light of the overhead chandeliers.

"I'm Delilah Smith, president of the Sherlock Holmes Society of Northern California," she announced, holding out her hand as if she were royalty.

"Nice to meet you." I took her hand and gave it a little shake.

"This," she gestured to the man, "is our vice president, Greg Timmons, and that," she gave a dismissive wave to a younger woman, "is Irene Reed."

Irene, wearing an elegant gown with lace trim, pearl buttons, and a bustle that could knock over a tea trolly, reached out to shake my hand. Her delicate fingers seemed as if they might break if I squeezed her hand too firmly. "Nice to meet you," she said, in a girlish voice. "I'm Irene Adler today. Isn't that perfect? Because my name is Irene." She glanced around the tearoom taking in her surroundings.

Jennifer appeared next to me, eyes wide with admiration for Irene's costume. "Your gown is lovely." Delilah cleared her throat, and Jennifer included her in her praise. "*Both* of your gowns are lovely. Very authentic. Are they vintage, or did you have them made?"

Delilah spoke before Irene could answer. "I'm wearing a backup costume I keep on hand. I usually lend it out to other members. That," she gestured to Irene, "is a custom-sewn gown I commissioned several years ago so I could embody the role of Irene Adler."

"The dry cleaner shrank it." Irene smoothed the fabric over her hips. "You wouldn't think that would happen, would you?"

Delilah huffed. "No, you wouldn't."

"Natural fibers will do that sometimes." Jennifer's eyes gleamed as she prepared to share all her knowledge about historical fashion. "Some people think they can get away with synthetic fabrics, but the trained eye can tell the difference."

"You are so right, dear." Delilah practically knocked

over Irene as she made her way to Jennifer, taking her by the arm and leaving the younger woman and Greg behind with me.

As Greg entered, he pulled an ornate pocket watch from his jacket and flipped it open, comparing it to his expensive wristwatch before tucking it away. "I parked my car in the driveway. I hope that's all right."

Before I could answer, Irene said, "Greg drove the Mercedes today. The Porsche wasn't big enough."

"Yes, that's fine," I said, amused by how proud she seemed of Greg's possessions. "Let me show you to the study."

"Luckily, I was available to step in as Irene Adler for the afternoon," Irene said as I showed her and Greg the way. "I love Sherlock Holmes, don't you? When I wear this dress, I feel like I'm a star in one of his movies."

We followed Jennifer and Delilah into the study.

"No, no, no. This will never do." Delilah waved her arms at my carefully chosen paintings. "Greg. Go get the paintings from the car. I'm so glad I brought them."

She turned to me with a condescending smile. "You've done a lovely job with this space, but authenticity is everything to our guests. They have paid a pretty penny to attend this fundraiser, and I owe them the proper attention to detail."

The doorbell rang again, and I hurried for the door. I recognized the couple dressed as Dr. and Mrs. Watson from their website photo. The man had a kind face partially hidden behind a thick mustache, while the woman beside him wore little makeup other than rosy blush on the apples of her cheeks and pale pink lipstick. A small top hat trimmed in midnight-blue velvet perched on top of her honey-brown updo.

I greeted them with, “Dr. Watson, I presume? And Mary Watson?”

“At your service.” The man removed his hat and bowed from the waist, then introduced himself and his partner. “I’m Todd, club historian, and this is Rosalie, our treasurer.”

“I’m April.” I opened the door wider and stepped aside for them to enter. “Welcome to SereniTea Tearoom.”

Rosemary entered and slowly took in the tearoom and its decor. “What a charming tearoom you have and such a lovely town. I can’t believe I’ve never visited before.”

“Serenity Cove is a bit of a secret,” I admitted. “There’s not much to do here other than sit and watch the waves crash on the shore. We don’t even have a full-service restaurant except for the one at the hotel, but they’re closed for renovations.”

As I led them to the tearoom, I had a feeling this would be an interesting afternoon.

CHAPTER 3

If I'd known Delilah Smith planned to redecorate my study like a one-woman bulldozer, I might have conveniently misplaced the reservation.

"No, no, no," she clucked as Greg struggled with a gilt-framed painting. "A little more to the left."

He did as he was told without complaint, sweat beading on his forehead. After the first oil painting was in place, he struggled to lift a second one, a heavy pastoral landscape from the 1860s featuring a suspiciously smug-looking goat. The painting was awkwardly proportioned and far too large for the wall, throwing off the balance of my carefully decorated room.

The scent of furniture polish and old books that normally filled the study was now competing with Delilah's overwhelming perfume, something floral and heavy that reminded me of funeral homes. It made my nose itch.

Delilah saw me watching and dramatically gestured at the tables I'd set with my best china. "These black napkins will never do. Don't you have something more appropriate?" She fingered the edge of one napkin as if it had personally offended her.

Jennifer, who'd been rearranging the table settings according to Delilah's instructions, shot me a wide-eyed look. Her usually cheerful face was strained, and I could tell she was reaching the limits of her patience.

"Why don't you get the other napkins to show Delilah, and I'll finish with the silverware." I gave her a look that said, *I'll handle this.*

Jennifer scurried from the room, obviously relieved to escape Delilah's criticisms. I cringed as Delilah ordered Greg to take down the landscape I'd recently hung there. The painting had been a splurge even before the restoration costs. "Can that one stay there, Delilah?" Thinking fast, I added, "It reminds me of the moors in England. I imagine *The Hound of the Baskervilles* might have been set in a similar area."

She gave me a long look, her eyes narrowing as she decided whether to accept my suggestion. Finally, she gave me a dismissive wave. "Fine. But I want the portrait of Queen Victoria over the fireplace. Nothing says 'Sherlock' like the monarch who reigned for his entire fictional life."

I nodded, not trusting myself to speak without showing my irritation. Back in the kitchen, I took a moment to breathe as Jennifer wisely set a cup of my favorite tea in front of me. I inhaled the soothing aroma of rose petals.

Irma paused making tea sandwiches long enough to say, "You didn't tell me Napoleon was invading the tearoom today. I would have brought my musket."

Jennifer looked up from slicing cucumbers. "You have a musket?"

"Doesn't everyone? I might have to go home and get it." Irma's deadpan delivery made it impossible to tell if she was joking. She cut crusts off the dainty sandwiches with surgical precision, her hands steady despite her years. After owning and running the Mermaid Café for four decades, she had the kind of efficiency that made her worth twice what I paid her. Maybe four times, since her wages consisted of all the food she could eat and an occasional bottle of wine she'd swipe from the pantry when she thought I wasn't watching.

"Delilah's not that bad." Jennifer couldn't help seeing the good side of everyone. "She's just... passionate."

Irma grunted, the sound expressing volumes of disagreement. "So was my Uncle Lloyd. He once tried to sue the city over a pothole shaped like Richard Nixon. Said it was insulting to the 37th president. Passion doesn't always lead to good things."

"I almost forgot," Jennifer said. "Delilah wants all the place cards rewritten in calligraphy. And she wants all the roses removed from the vases because she says they're hybrids that wouldn't have existed back in the nineteenth century. She does have a point about that."

I rubbed my temples, feeling the beginnings of a headache forming behind my eyes. "Okay, I'll let her know we don't have a calligrapher on the payroll and remove the offending roses from the flower arrangements. Anything else?"

The kitchen door swung open again, and Rosalie poked her head in. Unlike Delilah, her smile was warm and apologetic. "I hope we're not being too much trouble. Delilah tends to get enthusiastic."

"It's no trouble at all," I said smoothly. Running my tearoom had taught me to maintain a pleasant façade regardless of the chaos behind it.

She held up several linen bags tied with silk ribbons. "I brought some herbal tea blends as gifts for you and your team."

I perked up. "How kind of you."

"I'm an amateur herbalist." She handed them to me and pointed out the labels attached to the ribbons. "My grandmother taught me about herbs when I was a girl. There's a lavender-chamomile blend that helps with nerves, and a lemon-thyme that does wonders for sinus pressure, and a few of my other favorites. I'd love to hear what you think of them. My email is on the back of the labels."

I smelled the purple bag, and the scent of lavender caused my shoulders to relax. "What a lovely gift for the guests coming to your event."

She shook her head. "Oh, no. They didn't meet Delilah's standards. But I put together care packages for the other board members. Irene loves it when I bring her a bottle of headache tonic, though I suspect she likes the bottle more than what's inside."

Before I could say thank you, she slipped out of the

room. I followed her to the study where Delilah seemed only slightly miffed about the lack of a last-minute calligrapher. She seemed content with the room now that her paintings dominated the walls, the tables had been rearranged to her specifications, and the lights dimmed to provide the optimal lighting for their literary event.

Delilah led me to the opposite end of the room to the table she'd chosen for herself. "Rosalie will sit on my left to assist me. The others will sit at the other tables and act as table hosts to make sure that everyone is taken care of."

And here I thought that was my job. "I'll be in and out all afternoon," I assured her. "Along with Jennifer."

Right on cue, Jennifer entered with a newly rearranged vase and carried it over to Delilah for approval. After a long sigh, she decided they would do.

Irene and Greg stood a few feet away as if waiting for instructions. I wasn't sure if they were a couple in real life, but the way Irene stuck close to Greg, I suspected so. As Jennifer set the flowers on one of the tables, Irene asked her when food would be served.

Greg answered. "I think we're waiting for the other guests."

Irene snapped at him. "I knew that."

I had a feeling someone was hangry.

"We'll start serving as soon as Delilah gives the go ahead," Jennifer told Irene quietly. "Everything is ready to go. The best thing about afternoon tea, at least the way we serve it, is that all the food comes at once. You start from the bottom and eat your way to the top. The portions look small, but you'll be surprised how full you'll be when you get to the desserts."

The thought of desserts seemed to improve Irene's mood, but when Delilah called for Greg and he rushed off, she seemed to deflate.

I made my way over to her, hoping a little small talk might make her feel more comfortable. "It must be so fun to wear gorgeous gowns like the one you have on. Is that what attracted you to the group?"

"I'm a huge fan of Sherlock Holmes." Irene seemed to realize she should say more. "I've seen all the movies."

As she spoke, Jennifer returned with another vase and grinned. Probably because she'd never met an old movie she didn't like. "The ones with Basil Rathbone and Nigel Bruce are the best."

It took a moment for Irene to react. "Yes, I suppose. I like Robert Downey Jr., don't you?"

It was all I could do not to laugh at Jennifer's expression. It was as if someone had said, "I like polyester, don't you?" And anyone who knew her knew that she thought synthetic fibers were one of the worst inventions of all time.

"Also, I love the work we do to raise money for literacy programs," Irene added.

Greg returned to Irene's side. His dignified face softened when he spoke about the group's charity work. "It's important to give back. And literacy felt like the right fit for us. Books brought us together, so why not help others discover them too?"

Irene beamed. "Exactly! We raised money for a

summer reading program last year, and the turnout was incredible."

Delilah hovered closer. "It's a lot of work, organizing a gala. The rest of the group only sees the glamour, not the endless planning." The pride in her voice was unmistakable.

Rosalie, apparently the group's peacemaker, joined in. "All your hard work paid off, Delilah." Her gentle voice seemed to defuse the tension.

Delilah beamed. "Yes, well the important thing is helping the children and the illiterate." She patted Rosalie's shoulder. "Rosalie, dear, can you be a lamb and help Greg refold the programs? The corners don't line up and that won't do."

Rosalie hesitated for the tiniest moment before answering, "Yes, of course. Whatever you need me to do."

Irene rolled her eyes behind Delilah's back, a quick, subtle movement that I almost missed.

Irma looked up when we returned to the kitchen. "Everything going smoothly?"

Jennifer smirked. "Smooth as a gravel driveway."

"I think I'll stay in here," Irma said. "I'm not so good at holding my tongue."

"Really?" I somehow managed to keep from snickering. "I hadn't noticed."

The doorbell rang, and the paying guests for the event began to arrive. One mentioned the cost of the tickets, and I had to stop myself from gasping. The price seemed steep for tea and scones, even with my best clotted cream, but it was for a good cause after all.

I showed the first few arrivals into the study, where Delilah assured me that she would handle the seating arrangements.

When Jennifer and I returned with pots of tea, Delilah was in the middle of addressing the guests. "Ah, and here's our tearoom proprietress and her assistant now."

I gave the group a nod and a smile and set down the first teapots. Jennifer hurried back to the kitchen while I listened to Delilah speak.

"In the gold teapots, we have a Darjeeling tea, a black tea much like Sherlock Holmes might have drunk in his time." Delilah's booming voice carried across the room. "As you may know, if you've studied Sir Arthur Conan Doyle's stories as thoroughly as we have, the original stories do not specify a particular type or brand of tea that Holmes drank. However, tea is mentioned as part of daily life, particularly during consultations or while entertaining clients, reflecting typical Victorian habits rather than personal preference."

She paused, clearly enjoying being the center of attention. The guests watched her with varying degrees of interest, from rapt attention to polite boredom.

"I'm aware that some of you may prefer a tisane, that is, an herbal blend, and we have chosen one for you that combines chamomile, lemon balm, and a pinch of dried lavender buds. That is being served in the green pot. You'll also find sugar, honey, and that awful fake sweetener."

Several of the guests chuckled, and whether Delilah meant to be funny or not, she appeared pleased.

I held up my hand to get her attention.

"Yes, what is it?" Her tone suggested this had better be important.

"I wanted to let everyone know that if you run out of tea and would like more, remove the teapot lid and we'll be around to refill it the next time we pop in." I gave the guests a warm smile, which several returned. They seemed like a pleasant group, genuinely excited about the Holmes theme and the opportunity to spend an afternoon in period surroundings.

"Now," Delilah resumed addressing the room with barely a nod to acknowledge my contribution. "We shall have a quick Sherlock trivia contest before the food arrives."

Great. I hurried over to her and quietly said, "The trays are all ready to go. Would you like me to wait a few minutes before serving?"

She nodded. "You may serve the cordials now but wait at least ten minutes before you bring in the trays."

"Will do." I caught Todd's eye as I turned away, and he gave me a sympathetic smile. Obviously, I wasn't the only one who found Delilah challenging.

I shoved open the kitchen door and called out, "Time for the mocktails!"

We'd prepared the flutes ahead of time, filling them halfway with cranberry juice and a squeeze of lime juice over ice. Jennifer and Irma began topping them off with ginger ale while I garnished them with a lime wheel and mint sprig.

"They look so pretty," Jennifer said as we set them on trays and carried them into the other room, setting them in front of each guest.

Delilah paused her trivia quiz. "The Red-Headed League Cordials are a crimson, fizzing tribute to the cunning minds of Baker Street. And that takes us to our next trivia question. What was the *real* purpose of the Red-Headed League?" She paused dramatically, then read out the choices. "Was it A) to sponsor red-headed men in scholarly pursuits, B) to distract a shop owner while criminals dug a tunnel to a bank, C) to recruit men for a secret government mission, or D) to promote ginger hair dye in Victorian London?"

Out of curiosity, I dallied long enough to see if my guess was right, and it was. But then, B seemed the most obvious choice for a mystery story.

As I returned to the kitchen, all the tea trays were ready to go, stacked with scones, sandwiches, and mini quiches, and topped with adorable little desserts. For a moment, I forgot about Delilah's demanding presence.

This was why I'd left my high-pressure corporate job and sunk everything into this old house. It was for moments like this, when everything came together in a symphony of taste, smell, and sound. Even if some of the players, like Delilah, occasionally hit a sour note.

CHAPTER 4

If eavesdropping were an Olympic sport, Jennifer and I would have earned gold medals. As I went from table to table topping off teacups and refilling water glasses, I overheard Delilah whispering to Rosalie in the kind of tone people reserved for gossip or plotting a small coup.

"There's no reason the dress shouldn't have fit. Our guests must be so disappointed to see me in this poor excuse of a costume instead of in my rightful role as Irene Adler. Thank goodness I remembered my grandmother's heirloom brooch. It's the only thing that redeems this dress."

"It really does." Rosalie sounded reassuring but it was a bald-faced lie. It would take more than a brooch to make the dress appear anything other than drab and boring.

I moved closer to hear better, refilling water glasses along the way. The dynamics of this group fascinated me. Behind the polite exteriors and cosplay seemed to lurk some very modern resentments.

Delilah continued complaining. "I don't believe for a minute that it was the dry cleaner. Irene did something to the gown. I know it. I'm exactly the same size I have been since I married my dear, late husband. Donald encouraged me to watch my figure, and even though he's been gone for ten years, I've never put on even a pound."

Now *that* was interesting. I moved on to the next table to avoid being accused of eavesdropping, but I couldn't wait to get back in the kitchen and tell my friends what I'd heard. The Holmes Society suddenly became a lot more intriguing.

As I freshened the teapot at Todd's table, I noticed him watching Rosalie. She was helping an older guest select a sandwich from the tiered tray, laughing at something the woman said, completely unaware of Todd's gaze. His devotion was both touching and a little sad. I'd seen enough unrequited feelings in my tearoom to recognize the signs.

I'd experienced similar feelings myself years ago, before I'd learned that love shouldn't be a constant uphill struggle. My former fiancé had never quite looked at me the way Todd looked at Rosalie, which should have been my first clue that our relationship was doomed from the start. Sometimes I wondered if I'd ever find someone who looked at me that way, or if I was destined to remain the spinster tearoom owner, beloved by customers but going home to an empty house.

And then I met Sheriff Andrew Fontana. I felt an immediate attraction when he arrived to help rescue me from the tower of a local castle, but since he was married, I never acted on it. Even when he went through a divorce, I figured we'd never be more than friends. Turned out, starting out as friends was a great foundation for a relationship.

Irma took one look at me when I returned to the kitchen. "You look like you have something on your mind. Learn something interesting? Go on, spill."

I set down the empty teapot and leaned against the counter. "I think Todd is in love with Rosalie."

"Yes." Jennifer hurried over, wiping her hands on her apron. "That's obvious. Is that all?"

"Also, Delilah thinks Irene sabotaged her costume so she could be Irene Adler today."

Jennifer's eyes widened. "She didn't."

"I don't know if there's any truth to it. She claims she hasn't put on a pound since her husband died ten years ago, but did you see how much clotted cream she piled on her scones? I had to bring seconds. And there's not a single dessert left on her tray."

I wouldn't normally comment on someone's eating habits, but Delilah's hypocrisy bothered me. She expected perfection from everyone around her but herself.

"Did you hear what Irene told me?" Jennifer turned to Irma. "She thinks the movies with Robert Downey Jr. are the best when they have to be the worst Sherlock Holmes movies ever made. They're a travesty."

Irma shrugged. "I don't know about that. He's hot."

"And besides that," Jennifer continued, "I don't think Irene had ever even heard of Basil Rathbone or Nigel Bruce, even though they starred in *fourteen* Sherlock films." She gave us a sheepish look. "I suppose there's nothing wrong with that. Except when you claim to be a huge fan like she does."

"It did make me wonder," I agreed.

The gleam returned to Jennifer's eye. "My turn to make the rounds. I'll be back to spill the tea."

"Go for it." I felt a little guilty for encouraging her, but it seemed like harmless fun, and if it kept any of us from strangling Delilah, then more the better.

She grabbed the water pitcher and left Irma and me in the kitchen, where I took advantage of a few quiet moments to rest my feet. Irma didn't seem to be able to stop moving and said as much.

"I have two speeds. Go-go-go and stop. Besides, I can rest when I'm dead." She cast me a sideways glance. "Don't comment on that."

I shook my head. "All I was going to say was you're likely to outlive us all."

That put a rare smile on her face. "I might do that."

Jennifer returned with an empty pitcher and a grin that threatened to split her face.

I raised an eyebrow. "That didn't take long."

She leaned in, lowering her voice even though there was no one else in the kitchen. "Irene told Rosalie that Delilah is hinting she had the dress taken in out of jealousy. Irene said, and I quote, 'Just because she's eaten her way out of a corset doesn't make it my fault.'"

Irma cackled so hard, I had to shush her.

"Quiet. Someone might hear you."

She shrugged. "I remember at the Mermaid Café, how people wouldn't even notice me. The things I learned. And that was in my mermaid costume. Let me tell you, I turned heads back then."

"Back then?" I asked, raising an eyebrow. "Last year?"

"You have no idea how many men asked me out on dates when I wore that wig."

Figuring I might as well let her have her fantasies, I kept quiet.

Jennifer set a kettle on to boil. "It's so funny how people don't even seem to notice I'm around when I'm serving. I'm like furniture."

"Well, keep your ears open, Ms. Ottoman."

"Will do." Jennifer grabbed a plate and set several chocolate mousse mini tarts on it.

"Who are those tarts for?" I asked although I was pretty sure they were for Delilah.

"Who do you think?" Jennifer darted out of the kitchen, giggling to herself.

Irma shook her head. "That girl was born a century too late. She'd have made a fine lady's maid. Or a gossip columnist."

The next time Jennifer returned, she was practically skipping.

"The drama in this group." She set down two empty teapots. "Delilah wants these refilled."

Irma frowned. "Don't keep us in suspense."

"Give me a sec." She filled the pots with boiling

water, then took a seat at the kitchen island while they steeped.

"Greg told Irene that he's going to ask Rosalie to step down as treasurer. Said he found a bunch of 'errors' in her spreadsheet."

I refilled the kettle and put it back on the stove. "That doesn't sound like Rosalie, although I obviously don't know her."

Jennifer nodded. "Irene told him it must have been an honest mistake, and he should give Rosalie another chance."

"Good for her," I said, a little surprised that Irene would defend Rosalie.

Irma sniffed, her nose twitching like a suspicious rabbit. "I bet Rosalie's only mistake was questioning Greg's expenses."

"Oh, and get this." Jennifer lowered her voice to a whisper. "Greg said Rosalie's tonic that she gave to Irene is home-brewed moonshine."

"Interesting," Irma said. "So, Irene's a lush."

"Not necessarily," Jennifer said. "People say things all the time that aren't true."

"Anything else?" I asked. This was better than a soap opera.

"Well..." She sighed. "I feel a little guilty for gossiping."

"We're having a little harmless fun, that's all," Irma said. "Now spill it."

Jennifer dropped her voice to a whisper. "Delilah followed Irene and stopped her on the way to the ladies' room and said something like, 'If you don't tell him, I will.'"

"What did Irene say to that?"

Jennifer shrugged. "I didn't hear the rest, but I'm so curious who she meant."

"Me too. Though I'd bet my best teapot it's Greg. Those two have something going on between them."

Jennifer glanced at the clock. "How long do you think the event's going to go?"

"It's supposed to end at five, and it's... five fifteen." I sighed, realizing we were already running over. "I think it's time for us to start clearing plates, don't you? Hopefully they'll get the hint. If anyone asks for more tea and water, get it for them, but don't offer. If they ask for more food or desserts, tell them we're out."

"But we're not out." Jennifer couldn't even tell a little white lie without looking guilty. Her moral compass was permanently set to "completely honest," which made her a terrible poker player but a wonderful friend.

"Then it's cold, warm, stale, or whatever excuse you want to come up with." I wiped my hands on a towel. "Andy is planning to come over around seven, and I'd like to take a shower before he gets here."

The thought of seeing Andy brought a smile to my face. Between his work and my tearoom, we hadn't had much chance to spend time together. Tonight, we'd planned a quiet evening at home. No emergency calls, no distractions, and no interruptions.

Jennifer and I returned to the study where Delilah was announcing the winners of the trivia contest. Todd snapped pictures from the corner with all the enthusiasm of someone filing tax returns. He seemed to come to life when Rosalie came up to him.

"Delilah wants some more pictures of her with the guests," Rosalie whispered.

He frowned. "Of course she does."

The trivia contest wrapped up with Delilah handing out prizes. For the grand prize winner, she presented a magnifying glass on a chain that could double as a necklace or a weapon, depending on how spirited things got. She had enough pins, bookmarks, and other novelty items so that no one left empty-handed.

"Thank you all for coming," Delilah announced with a proud smile. "We hope to see you again at our next gathering. Please check our website for our upcoming event calendar and make sure to join our mailing list, if you haven't already."

The guests began to trickle out, chatting happily. As I stood outside the study door, thanking the guests for coming, Delilah emerged.

"Another successful event." She sighed as if she'd done all the work herself.

"I'm glad you think so," I said, surprised to get any praise at all. Still, I'd hosted enough events to recognize the glassy-eyed fatigue of someone who had been "on" for too many hours.

"I wonder." She took hold of my arm. "Might I rest somewhere for a few minutes while the others take care of packing things up."

"Oh." I hesitated, but my sympathy won over. "I'll

take you to the upstairs parlor. There's a sofa and a recliner. Are you feeling okay?"

"Jush a little tired."

And a little drunk? Had she had some of Rosalie's tonic? Her words slurred slightly, and her grip on my arm tightened.

"I'll show you the way."

It was a slow climb up the grand staircase, and I was running low on patience. We still had a lot to do, and cleanup would be easier and faster after they left. If they ever did.

"My only disappointment was seeing Irene in my gown." She stopped to catch her breath. "Maybe… I am a little jealous."

I didn't know what to say to that, so instead, I coaxed her up the last few stairs.

"Thash what people say."

"Oh, I'm sure they don't. The room is down the hall this way." I guided her past the bedrooms to the parlor at the front of the house.

"Greg comforted me when I lost my husband. And when his wife died last year after a long illness..."

I began to get the picture. "You thought you and he would be together."

She nodded, her perfectly coiffed hair bobbing slightly. "How am I supposed to compete with a thirty-year-old?"

"You don't." I felt uncomfortable with her confiding in me, so I cut the conversation short. "Okay, here we are. You're sure you're okay? Need anything?"

She plopped onto the sofa. "I'll resh for a bit, and I'll be..." Her voice trailed off.

"Right as rain?" I suggested.

"Huh?"

"Okay then. Have a nice rest."

I closed the door behind me so the noise from downstairs wouldn't disturb her and hurried downstairs to start cleaning up. Most of the paying guests had left, but Greg, Irene, Rosalie, and Todd stayed behind.

Greg looked up when I entered. "You don't mind if we have another cup of tea before we put things back the way we found them."

He hadn't even bothered to make it sound like a question. Yes, I minded. I'd been on my feet since dawn, and all I wanted was for the day to be over so my evening could start.

"If you don't mind us cleaning up around you." I managed to keep my tone pleasant. After stacking as many plates as I could, I grabbed a tiered tray with my free hand. "I'll have Jennifer bring you more tea."

Irma took the plates from me as I entered the kitchen. She'd been on her feet since noon yet somehow remained as energetic as ever.

"Why don't you sit down?" I suggested. "You must be tired."

"If I sit down, I won't get back up."

I chuckled. "I can live with that. Jennifer and I can finish up here if you want to head home. I truly appreciate your help today."

"Well in that case..." She poured herself a mug of tea

and took a seat at the island. "If it's alright with you, I think I'll hang around a little longer and see if there's any more drama. Are your events always so rocky?"

Jennifer entered with a handful of napkins. "I think it was pretty smooth."

"Smooth as a gravel driveway," I said, repeating Jennifer's words from earlier.

Irma grinned. "That good, huh?"

I nodded. "Considering I managed not to murder Delilah, I'm calling the event a success."

CHAPTER 5

Jennifer gasped. "Murder is nothing to joke about, April."

"Sorry. You're right. I should know better." I headed back to the study with a fresh pot of Darjeeling, because apparently this party had no end time.

Rosalie emerged as I reached the doorway, her purse over her shoulder, and almost ran into me.

"Are you leaving *already*?" I didn't mean to be snarky, but somehow it came out that way. Luckily, she didn't notice.

"I don't drive after dark anymore. My night vision's terrible." She reached out and took my hand. "Thanks for a lovely event. You did a great job. Especially—"

"Wait, Rosalie," Greg interrupted as he appeared behind her, startling both of us. "I'll walk you to the door."

Her expression was unreadable, but the way she

turned to leave without acknowledging him spoke volumes. He chased after her, obviously not getting the message.

I entered the study and set the pot of tea in front of Irene and Todd who were deep in conversation. The portrait of Queen Victoria seemed to watch disapprovingly from above the fireplace.

Todd looked up. "Have you seen Rosalie?"

"Yes, she said she's leaving."

"Now?" He pushed his chair away from the table and stood, but Irene grabbed his arm.

"Are you leaving, too?" she asked, her voice taking on a pleading tone that seemed at odds with her usual self-assurance.

"Yeah, as soon as I grab all my stuff."

"You can't go yet. You know Delilah won't be happy if..."

I didn't find out what Delilah wouldn't be happy about, because I left the room. I'd grown tired of the group and their petty squabbles.

As I passed through the tearoom on the way to the kitchen, I saw Rosalie hadn't managed to leave yet. I heard Greg say, "Don't say anything to Delilah."

I wasn't trying to eavesdrop this time, truly, but if the universe insisted on dropping suspicious statements directly in my path, who am I to ignore them?

Rosalie tilted her head. "Or what?"

There was a challenge in her voice I hadn't heard before. The soft-spoken treasurer suddenly seemed harder and more forceful.

Before Greg could answer, Todd appeared, nearly

colliding with the sideboard. "Rosalie, wait up. I'll walk you to your car."

Rosalie's expression softened when she saw him. Whatever tension had been crackling between her and Greg seemed to dissolve as she took Todd's offered arm. "Thank you. That would be lovely."

Something passed between Greg and Rosalie, an unspoken communication, a warning perhaps, before she turned away. Greg stood frozen for a moment, his fingers tapping against his thigh in an agitated rhythm before he retreated back to the study.

Back in the kitchen, I told Irma and Jennifer that at least one of the board members had left. My shoulders ached from the long day of serving, and I was looking forward to changing into something more comfortable.

"I'll go and see if I can hurry them up at all," Jennifer said. "Nothing like someone taking away your teaspoon to let you know the tea party is over."

"I'll join you." Irma stood. "Maybe if I run the vacuum cleaner, they'll really get the message."

I sank onto a stool and leaned my elbows on cool tile of the island, grateful for the momentary break. The kitchen was quiet with only the hum of the refrigerator and the ticking vintage wall clock.

Minutes later, Jennifer returned to the kitchen with Todd who thanked us for all our hard work.

"It's our pleasure," Jennifer gushed, her perpetual enthusiasm somehow still intact after the long day.

"I've got a podcast interview early tomorrow," he said as if we'd asked for an explanation.

"Podcast?" I asked, trying to sound mildly curious

although I wasn't really. The last thing I needed was another conversation starter.

"Tomorrow's episode is a big one. Possibly my most important yet."

"About the Sherlock Society?" I wondered how many people listened to podcasts about literary fan clubs.

His smile was self-satisfied. "You'll have to wait until it airs to find out." He swept out of the kitchen, tripping on the door sill and attempting to recover with an awkward bow.

Irma grabbed a wine glass and a bottle of chardonnay from the refrigerator. I was about to ask if I could join her, when she reminded me I had a date.

"It's not a date," I said, not sure why I was explaining. "We're going to hang out and maybe watch a movie."

She waved me away. "Go on upstairs. We've got it handled. You'd better hurry, though. That sheriff of yours shows up looking like Mr. Darcy again, and someone else might steal him."

"I almost forgot about Delilah." I sighed. "I'll check on her before I get in the shower."

As I stood to go upstairs, the ground shuddered then rolled and I grabbed onto the island.

"Earthquake!" Jennifer yelped as she hurried to the doorway and held on.

Cups rattled in the sink, and plates and tea trays fell from the counter. The pendant light above us swung back and forth. I cringed at the sound of things crashing, thudding and shattering coming from the other room. The lights flickered once, twice, and then everything went dark, or semi-dark, since we still had another two hours or so of sunlight peeking through the curtains.

Living in California for all of my fifty years, I'd experienced my share of earthquakes, but this one was strong enough to make my heart pound. I waited for the shaking to stop, hoping the damage to my home, furnishings, and teacups would be minimal.

"That was a big one," Irma said as the shaking came to a stop. "About 7.2, and fairly close, maybe ten or twenty miles from here if I know my earthquakes, and I do. Hopefully the epicenter is out to sea, because if it was inland, there's going to be some serious damage."

Jennifer and I stared at her.

"What are you? The earthquake whisperer?" I asked, my voice slightly higher than normal from the adrenaline still coursing through my system.

She grinned like I'd paid her a huge compliment. "Yeah, you might say so. It's a gift."

I was about to go check on the others when Greg and Irene burst through the kitchen door.

"Oh, good. You're okay." Greg's voice trembled. "We thought we should check on you."

"Where's Delilah?" Irene asked, glancing around the kitchen as if expecting to find the society president hiding behind the island.

"She's upstairs resting. I was about to go check on her when everything started shaking."

"I wonder how long the power will be out." Greg seemed nervous, but maybe he'd never been in a major earthquake before. "Do you think the streetlights are out too? Maybe we should get on the road before it gets dark."

"7.3!" Irma called out triumphantly from the other room, where she was checking her phone. "Nailed it." She held up her phone showing us the seismic website.

"I'll go get the flashlights in case the power stays out for a while." Jennifer headed for the closet. "And candles. Do we still have those little ones in teacups?"

"Let's only light the candles if we absolutely have to," I said. "Nothing says 'tragedy' like setting a historic home on fire during an aftershock."

"Aftershock?" Greg's face became even paler.

As if on cue, the ground began to move again, and he looked like he was about to bolt.

"Doorway!" Jennifer barked in a commanding tone I'd never heard from her. She slipped into the space between the kitchen and the pantry area and held onto both door jambs. "It's the safest place to be."

Greg obeyed, and he and Irene stood in the other doorway that led to the front room. They looked every bit the couple in a rom-com who had been forced to be very close and were trying hard not to kiss.

The aftershock, a mild one, was over quickly, and Jennifer began digging around in the back room. She returned moments later, her arms full of flashlights, battery-powered lanterns, and a few slightly dusty candles in decorative holders shaped like teacups.

I handed a flashlight to Irene. "Can you check on Delilah? The parlor is the room at the front of the house."

"I'll go with you," Greg called out after her, but she was already halfway up the stairs.

Irma pointed her flashlight toward the back door. "I'll go around the house and see if there's any major damage."

"I'll stay right here and pretend all of the fragile items we have on every level surface of the tearoom are just fine and nothing's been broken, cracked, or shattered." The crashing sounds I'd heard earlier told me otherwise, but I wasn't ready to face the truth.

Jennifer nodded. "I'd rather not think about what we're going to have to clean up. Oh! I hope Rosalie's okay. I wonder how far she got before the quake. It would be scary to be in a car when the ground starts shaking."

"Todd's on the road too. I hope they both make it home okay." I meant it, but I was more worried about things closer to home. "For the moment, I'm going to be selfish and think about myself and my teapot collection and how long we have before everything in the refrigerator and freezer goes bad."

From upstairs, Irene's voice called out, "Greg?" followed by, "You might want to come up here."

Jennifer and I grabbed flashlights and hurried after Greg. I nearly stopped in my tracks when I saw what had become of my tidy, perfectly arranged tearoom. Floor lamps lay on their side. Shards of china teacups, teapots, and decorative jars littered the floor along with loose tea. I'd have quite a clean-up job, but it would have to wait a bit.

Greg and Jennifer were already halfway up the

stairs, so I hurried after them. As we reached the second floor, my stomach fluttered.

Because if there's one thing I've learned, it's this: When someone says, "You might want to come up here," it's never because they've found extra scones.

CHAPTER 6

The parlor door was open, and inside, Irene crouched beside the vintage floral sofa.

"She won't wake up," she said in a voice barely above a whisper. "I—I think something's wrong."

I hurried past Greg, my flashlight beam jittering over furniture until it landed on Delilah.

She was sprawled on the sofa, her legs tucked primly to one side, one hand resting in her lap, the other draped over the arm like she'd posed herself for a sentimental portrait. Her eyes were closed, her face oddly peaceful.

Too peaceful.

The air in the room felt strangely thick, as if time itself had slowed down. Outside, the last fading light of day cast long shadows across the walls, making the familiar room seem suddenly alien.

Irene stood, and I took her place, although my knees didn't like kneeling much. Setting my flashlight on the table, I reached for her wrist hoping to feel a flutter of life beneath my fingers. Her skin felt cool. Too cool. I touched the side of her neck where the carotid artery should have been pulsing strongly.

Still nothing.

"Call for an ambulance," I said to Jennifer, even though I was almost positive it was too late. The sinking feeling in my stomach told me we were dealing with something much worse than a fainting spell.

Jennifer pulled her cell from her pocket and dialed. We all heard the obnoxious buzzing that emanated from her phone followed by the message, "All circuits are busy. Try your call later."

Irene's face contorted as she looked from Jennifer back to me. "But we need to get help for her. Now. There must be a way."

"We'll keep trying," I said gently. "But I'm sorry to tell you…she doesn't have a pulse."

"What do you mean?"

"I think she's gone."

"No!" She threw herself into Greg's arms and sobbed.

Greg patted her back helplessly. He blinked rapidly, staring down at Delilah like he expected her to sit up and start scolding us for not fluffing the sofa cushions.

"I told her to take it easy," he stammered. "She's had heart issues for a few years now. She takes medication, but maybe she thought she didn't need it anymore."

Irene pulled back from Greg and wiped the tears from her cheeks with trembling fingers. "Remember how tired she was? I told her we should call a doctor, but she said she was fine. It was almost as if she knew it was her time."

Jennifer and I exchanged a glance. No woman in her fifties thinks it's her time, not without a doctor telling her so. Even then they're likely to think they can beat the odds.

Something about Delilah's expression made the hairs on my arms stand up. Peaceful, yes. But maybe too peaceful.

We all stood in a stunned circle around the body of the woman who had bossed us around for the better part of the day and then calmly died in my upstairs parlor.

At last, I said the only thing that came to mind. "At least she didn't suffer."

Although the way she'd acted earlier, tipsy and slurring her words, I couldn't help but wonder. Wouldn't she have clutched her chest? Cried out? Done something more dramatic than this peaceful pose, like a middle-aged Sleeping Beauty waiting for Prince Charming to wake her?

"Had she been drinking?" I asked Irene.

Greg answered. "She never drank. Said it showed moral weakness."

But then why had I thought she seemed tipsy? "Maybe it was a stroke that came on so suddenly she didn't even realize what was happening."

I pulled out my own phone to call Freddie. What good was it having a doctor and county coroner for a friend if you couldn't call them when you found a dead body? I got the same screeching noise and message as Jennifer had.

"This is why people shouldn't make unnecessary calls in an emergency," I muttered under my breath.

Downstairs, a man's voice called out, "Greg? Irene? Where is everyone?"

It was Todd. I thought he'd be halfway home by now. Had he come back to check on his friends?

"We'll be right down," Greg called.

I followed the others into the hallway and closed the door. The least I could do for Delilah was preserve her dignity. Todd came bounding up the stairs, clearly not noticing our solemn mood.

"There's been an earthquake!" he said, as if he were the first to break the news.

"Yes, we noticed," Greg said in a monotone. "And besides that—"

"A rockslide completely blocked the road." Todd's frustration was understandable, but he seemed almost panicky. "I keep trying to figure out how to get out of town, but my phone won't give me an alternate route."

"Because there is no alternate route," I said. "There's only one way in and out of Serenity Cove."

Greg tried again. "Todd, there's something—"

"But I need to get home. Tonight."

Greg grabbed him by his arms. "Todd. There's something I have to tell you. Delilah is dead."

He stared at Greg for a long moment. "What are you talking about?" His gaze went to Irene then to me and back to Greg.

"It was her heart," Irene said. "It just gave out."

He turned to me. "Is it true?"

"I'm sorry to say, yes. We found her just a few minutes ago. In there." I gestured to the parlor. I can let you see her if it would help." I hoped it might make it seem more real for him.

He nodded, and I led him to the parlor door, pushing it open. He took one step inside the room, and I waited for the truth to sink in. He reemerged looking shaken.

I closed the door behind him as the house began to rock. Greg grabbed the railing while Jennifer and Irene shared the doorway to one of the bedrooms. This aftershock was milder and ended in seconds.

Greg seemed reluctant to let go. "How many aftershocks are there going to be?"

"It's hard to know." It had been decades since I'd been in a major earthquake. "But they should slow down and get weaker."

Irma's voice came from downstairs. "Hey! Where'd everybody go?"

"We'll be down in a minute," I yelled back, then turned to the others. "Why don't we all go downstairs while we figure things out."

"Figure what out?" Todd asked. "Why we've suddenly become extras in some disaster movie?"

"Feels more like horror to me," Greg grumbled.

"I've always wanted to be on the big screen," Irene said. "But this is definitely not the kind of movie I had in mind."

Todd stopped me as the others went ahead. "There's really only one way out of town?"

"Unless you have a boat or want to hike over Mount Tumble."

Todd blinked. "Mount what?"

"It's more of a hill, really. Wait a sec." My pulse quickened. "Your phone is working? Of course. Even with the phone lines jammed, we can access the internet." I turned to Jennifer. "Right?"

She nodded. "As long as one or both of the cell towers are standing."

Todd frowned. "This town only has two cell towers? And only one way out of town?" He leaned against the banister and sighed. "I need to get home to get ready for tomorrow's podcast."

While Todd trudged downstairs to join the others, I pulled Jennifer aside. "Can you do that thing where you call someone using the internet?"

She brightened. "Why didn't I think of that? But I'm not sure we'll be able to get through to emergency services."

"I'd rather call Freddie anyway."

I handed Jennifer my phone, and she showed me how to make the call. Soon, I heard Freddie's voice come through loud and clear.

"April, are you okay? Is everyone okay?"

"Almost everyone. One of our guests passed away."

"Oh, April." Her sigh came through the line. "Another body in the tearoom?"

"Not in the tearoom. In the upstairs parlor." That didn't really help, but I wanted her to have accurate information. "She was feeling tired and went up to rest. When we checked on her after the earthquake, she was gone. No pulse, and she was cool to the touch. The people with her say she had heart issues."

"You say she was tired. Any other symptoms?"

I told her about Delilah's slurred speech and slow movements. "I thought she'd been drinking, but the others insist she never drinks."

Freddie was quiet for a moment. Then she said, "That doesn't sound at all like a heart attack. Maybe a stroke. Did she mention weakness on one side? Did she seem confused?"

"No, not really. You should have seen her, Freddie. She looked so peaceful lying there, with a calm, almost serene expression. And let me tell you, I doubt anyone saw that expression on her face before today."

"That's odd," Freddie said.

The phone was silent for several seconds and I'd almost thought we'd lost the connection until Freddie spoke again.

"You might not be dealing with natural causes."

I groaned. "Not again."

CHAPTER 7

Freddie's voice was soothing, though her words were not. "They're hoping to send a crew out in the morning to clear the road. As soon as I get the word, I'll come straight there."

"In the morning?" I repeated, trying not to panic. I turned to Jennifer. "Why don't you wait for me downstairs?"

After she was gone, I lowered my voice so the others wouldn't overhear me. "Freddie, I have a dead body in my upstairs parlor."

"I know you're upset, April, but we've got power lines down, a section of highway that's completely buckled, and half the county without electricity."

"I'm in a house with no power with a dead body and three strangers. And if Delilah's death was not due to natural causes, as you suspect, then one of those three strangers could be a murderer." My voice cracked as the reality hit me again.

"Oh, that is a problem." After a meaningful pause, she asked, "Who's with you beside the three strangers?"

"Irma and Jennifer."

"Stay together at all times. I'll see if I can get an officer out to the house."

What a nightmare. "And what about the dead body?"

She softened her voice. "Leave her where she is. Cover her with a sheet, lock the door, turn the heat off in that room, and wear gloves if you touch her."

"Why in the world would I touch her?"

Freddie ignored the question. "And take pictures."

"Pictures?" I asked, blinking. The incongruity of it struck me, documenting death in the same room where I'd done my taxes. "For what? Her online memorial page?"

"To send to me. It probably was a stroke or heart failure. Have you called Sheriff Fontana?"

"I was going to call him next."

I disconnected and leaned against the wall feeling defeated. My home had always been my refuge. Now it felt like a trap, its familiar creaks somehow ominous without electrical hums to mask them.

Andy's phone rang four times. "April! Are you all right?"

"Yes, but—"

"Is Jennifer with you?"

"Yes, but—"

"Did you have a lot of damage?"

"Not really, but—"

"Thank goodness. The whole county's a mess. Bridges are unstable, power's out in several towns, and we don't even know the full extent of the damage. We won't for days. I'll call as soon as I can." Click.

I stared at my phone as Irma bounded upstairs. "That good, huh? Do you really have a dead body in your parlor?"

Fighting back tears, I managed to say, "Freddie thinks Delilah's death might not have been natural. She can't get here until tomorrow. And Andy hung up before I could tell him what happened."

She patted my arm. "We'll get through this together. Now buck up, 'cause you've got people downstairs getting restless."

"Please tell me I'm not stuck with them all night."

"Okay, I won't tell you. Let's go downstairs, raid the refrigerator, and figure things out."

Greg, Irene, and Todd stopped their heated discussion when they saw me. "Any news about the road?" Greg asked.

"The road won't be open until tomorrow."

"Tomorrow!" Todd looked like he wanted to kick a wall.

"There's a hotel in town, right?" Irene asked hopefully.

"It's closed for renovations." I wanted to tell them I didn't like the situation any more than they did, but then I thought of Sarah, the owner of Serenity Cove Bed and Breakfast. "I'll call the B&B for you. I'm sure they have rooms. It's the off-season, after all."

I made the call.

"April!" she answered, sounding out of breath. "You okay?"

"Physically? Yes. Mentally? On the verge. Please tell me you've got a few rooms."

"Oh, sweetie, with the hotel closed, we've been booked every day this month. Every bed in every room is taken."

I groaned, my last hope evaporating. "Do you have any space at all? A screened porch? A linen closet with good airflow?"

"Not even a closet. I'm so sorry."

I disconnected the call, and didn't even pretend to be happy to be stuck with them. "I guess we'll have to make the best of it."

Back in the kitchen, I grabbed the spoon Irma held out and dug into the chocolate mousse I'd made yesterday. Jennifer pushed open the door and collapsed on a stool at the island, laying her cheek against the cool tile.

"Better get another spoon," I said to Irma.

Irma handed a spoon to Jennifer, and we finished the bowl in record time. I half expected Irma to lick the bowl.

"Irma, could you take in a guest or two?"

"Absolutely not."

"Someone can take my room, and I'll stay at Irma's," Jennifer offered.

Irma looked scandalized. "You most certainly will not."

Jennifer crossed her arms, showing backbone for a change. "You said I could stay if there was ever an emergency. This qualifies, doesn't it?"

"There's no way we're leaving April here alone with a possible murderer," Irma said, her voice softening.

Jennifer let her arms fall to her sides. "Oh. I hadn't thought of that."

I glanced at my phone's shrinking battery and reluctantly powered it off. With nightfall approaching, my familiar home would soon be filled with ominous shadows.

"I suppose there's no point crying over a dead body and extra mouths to feed." I straightened my shoulders. I'd have to keep my guests warm, fed, and distracted until help arrived, while making sure none had the opportunity to destroy evidence or harm anyone else.

"We'll help," Jennifer said cheerfully.

Irma reluctantly agreed. "I suppose we'll need to inventory the candles and see what we can cook on that old gas range of yours."

"Thank goodness it's not electric." At least I had something to be thankful for.

"Whatever would you do, April May," Irma teased, "if you couldn't put the kettle on and brew a pot of tea?"

I shook my head. "That would be a sad, sad day indeed."

CHAPTER 8

I rummaged through the refrigerator like a contestant on "Disaster Dinner," pulling out cold cuts, cheese, half a quiche, and pickled beets from someone who probably hated me.

Then I thought about my walk-in freezer full of frozen pot pies, soup, and desserts. If the power stayed out, I'd have to throw everything out.

"Today we feast!" I announced, carrying frozen items to the counter. "Tomorrow, we won't have an excuse to eat like we all got dumped by our boyfriends."

Jennifer held a stack of blankets that reached up to her chin. Only the tips of her ballet flats and the top of her ponytail were visible. "We've got enough bedding for everyone to sleep downstairs."

"They can fight over the sofas. Greg might need the air mattress."

While the trio paced and complained, I cooked. It

felt normal. I told Irma and Jennifer about the things Chef Emile would complain about.

"*Sacré bleu!*" I said in a cartoonish French accent. "Zee soup! You will burn it, you silly woman."

"You still miss him, don't you," Jennifer said. "Even if he did complain a lot."

"I do. Hardly a day goes by when I don't think about him."

We laid out the food buffet-style. The three guests hurried over, filling their plates.

"I'll eat in the kitchen," Jennifer said tentatively.

"Me too." Irma followed Jennifer with her overloaded plate.

"Enjoy your dinner," I told the guests, then joined my friends.

Irma opened wine, and I grabbed glasses. "Just a little for me," Jennifer said.

"How are the ungrateful dinner guests?" Irma asked.

"They've had a shock. They're stuck overnight with the choice of our sofas or the floor."

"They could sleep in their cars," Irma said. "You're too soft."

Jennifer interrupted. "She's being kind. Maybe you should try it."

Irma gasped, then grinned. "Good for you. I like seeing you stand up to people."

I followed Jennifer into the other room where our guests accepted glasses of wine. I sat with them, trying to learn more about them.

"What drew you to the Holmes Society?"

Greg's face lit up. "I've been a Holmesian since

childhood. Read *The Hound of the Baskervilles* at nine and was hooked. Did you know Doyle killed Holmes off because he wanted to focus on 'serious' writing? He got so much hate mail he brought Holmes back."

Irene cleared her throat. "I love how logical he is. 'Elementary, my dear Watson.'"

Todd winced, and I could guess why. Even I knew that famous phrase never actually appeared in Doyle's stories, but I wasn't about to correct her.

"What's your favorite story?" I asked.

"*The Hound of the Baskervilles.* I like stories with dogs," Irene said confidently.

Todd nearly spit out his wine.

Greg leaned forward with the fervor of a man about to launch into a well-rehearsed monologue. "Most people don't realize how spiritual Doyle was. After he lost his son in World War I, he became deeply involved in the spiritualist movement—séances, mediums, the whole bit. Which is ironic considering how rational Holmes always was."

"Ironic," I repeated, though the word felt inadequate.

The conversation stalled, so I returned to the kitchen where Irma had opened a second bottle.

She held up her glass. "Considering the day we've had, I didn't think you'd mind."

"I don't mind at all." I planned to stop after one glass, since I didn't know what the night had in store for us.

Jennifer had assembled a platter of desserts that felt

like offerings at a wake. She offered Irma a mini eclair. "I think they're yummier half-frozen anyway."

I took the platter from her. "I'll take this to the others, and you grab the ice cream. We might as well eat it before it melts."

When I returned to the dining room with the tray of desserts, Greg had abandoned his seat and was pacing near the fireplace like a caged animal. The restless energy that had been building in him all evening seemed to have reached a breaking point.

He turned when he saw me, his eyes bright with an idea that I immediately distrusted. "You know what might help us all sleep better tonight?"

I hesitated, setting the platter down carefully and waiting to hear his suggestions.

"A séance." He beamed like he'd invented it himself. "Like Sir Arthur Conan Doyle might have had. We could make contact with the spirit realm and maybe get some answers about what happened here today. We might even be able to connect with Delilah's spirit."

"No way." I turned to face him fully, hands on my hips. "Absolutely not. I forbid it."

He seemed surprised and even offended by my reaction, as though I wasn't allowed to make the rules in my own home. "You forbid it?"

"Yes. Forbid, prohibit, veto, ban..." I'd run out of synonyms, but not out of outrage. "In other words, there will be no séance in my house. Not tonight and not ever."

Greg folded his arms over his chest, his enthusiasm transforming into stubborn defiance. "But what if

Delilah is trying to tell us something? What if her spirit is trapped here, unable to rest?"

"I'm willing to live with that possibility." I gave him a look intended to say I wasn't kidding. "Now the three of us are going upstairs to get ready for bed. I put extra towels in the downstairs bathroom and some toiletry items. You're welcome to anything in the kitchen." Why not, since I'd probably have to throw most of it out if the power stayed out much longer.

Jennifer and Irma seemed more than ready to call it a night, but I could see Jennifer's hesitation when her eyes drifted to the ceiling. The thought of sleeping alone with a dead body at the end of the hall was clearly weighing on her mind, and I didn't blame her.

"Do you snore?" Irma asked with characteristic bluntness.

"No," Jennifer said uncertainly. "I don't think so."

"Well, I do, but you're welcome to share a room with me if one of the rooms has two beds. I have a California King bed at home so I can stretch out when I sleep, but I suppose I can make an exception for one night."

This was vintage Irma—gruff on the surface but generous underneath, though she'd never admit it.

"Yes, my room has two beds." Jennifer sounded relieved to not have to be alone in her room. "Do you think we should offer the guest bedroom to Irene? It seems wrong to make her sleep on the sofa when we have a perfectly good bed available."

"That would be the right thing to do, I suppose." I paused to think it over, weighing hospitality against practicality, then shook my head. "We'd better leave it empty in case Irma's snoring keeps you awake."

We said goodnight and headed up the stairs, retreating to our rooms. The house settled into an uneasy hush. Without the electrical hum that usually masked my home's nighttime noises, every creak and groan seemed amplified. Wind rattled the windows and somewhere in the distance, a tree groaned eerily.

As I clicked off my flashlight and settled into bed, I told myself the road would reopen in the morning, and Freddie and Andy would arrive and find out what happened to Delilah. If she'd had a heart attack, we'd laugh later about how we worried about spending the night with a murderer under the same roof.

But even as I had the thought, I knew we wouldn't laugh about a woman's death.

In the darkness, I lay awake listening to the house breathe around me waiting for the morning light and whatever truths it might reveal.

CHAPTER 9

My eyes blinked open in the dark room without so much as the glowing numbers from my bedside clock for light. The events of the day came flooding back in a rush.

Voices drifted up from downstairs, muffled but distinct enough to penetrate the old house's wooden floors. My heart began to beat faster, that immediate spike of adrenaline that comes with unexpected sounds in the dark, and then I remembered our overnight guests. I should have given them a curfew or at least set some ground rules about being considerate to their sleeping hosts. Too late now.

The moonless sky outside my bedroom window showed no hint that dawn was coming soon, so I closed my eyes and willed myself back to sleep. That didn't work. The voices were hushed, but whispers in the dark were hard to ignore. Without power, I couldn't depend on the fan for white noise or play soothing sounds on my phone.

Being awakened before dawn always made me cranky under the best of circumstances, and these were decidedly not the best of circumstances. After what felt like an hour but was probably closer to five minutes, I gave up on sleep. I threw the covers aside, ready to stomp downstairs and chew them out when I paused. What exactly would I say to them? "Excuse me, but you're whispering too loud?" Their whispers meant they were at least trying to be considerate.

But when the voices got louder, I grabbed my flashlight from the nightstand, muttering under my breath, "Is a good night's sleep so much to ask after the day we've had?"

The stairs creaked beneath my weight. Every groan and protest of the old timber seemed amplified in the still air. As I reached the bottom step, I shone my flashlight around the empty room.

No one was in the tearoom, where I was reminded of the cleanup that awaited me in the morning, nor were they in the sitting area by the fireplace. I crept toward the kitchen, my flashlight beam dancing ahead of me, only to find it empty except for the remnants of whatever midnight snack my guests had helped themselves to. Crumbs on the counter, an open jar of jam, plates left carelessly by the sink. It hadn't occurred to me to establish house rules about cleaning up after themselves.

The door to the study was half open, and as I approached, drawn by the soft murmur of voices, I stopped dead in my tracks.

Irene, Greg, and Todd sat around a table in the center of the room with their hands joined, their faces lit by the flickering glow of candles that cast dancing shadows on the walls. The scene had an otherworldly quality.

Greg spoke in a hushed, reverent voice that carried the weight of someone who believed he was making contact with the beyond. "If you are here Delilah, tap once for yes."

And then *someone* tapped once on the table. The sound was sharp and clear in the quiet room, and the three mortals gasped in unison, their eyes wide with wonder.

"She *is* here," Irene said in a hushed tone.

In the dim light, I couldn't be sure, but Todd seemed amused. Was he playing a trick on the others or was he in on the joke?

Greg called out, "Delilah, we need to know if your soul is at peace."

"What do you think you're doing?" I asked, and three pairs of wide eyes turned in my direction.

"We've contacted Delilah's spirit," Irene answered, sounding even more childlike than usual.

"No, you haven't. I've never known a ghost who could..." I stopped before I gave away my ghost whisperer abilities. "I thought I made it clear to you, Greg, that I did not want a séance happening in my home." I kept my voice low, so I didn't wake Irma and Jennifer, though it took considerable effort not to shout. "And this is how you repay my hospitality? I should throw you out on the street right now and let you sleep in your cars."

"But they insisted," Greg protested, gesturing helplessly at Irene and Todd, who looked like children caught raiding the cookie jar. "And Delilah is definitely here, or at least she was until you interrupted us. She made contact with us."

"No, you weren't. Todd is playing a trick on you."

Todd shrugged. "I was just having a little harmless fun."

"Fun?" Irene stood, and even in the dim light I could see her red face. "I was freaked out. I thought Delilah was here and she was going to…" She didn't finish her sentence and instead stormed out of the room.

I pinched the bridge of my nose, feeling a tension headache threaten to return. "We'll deal with this in the morning. Out of the room!"

Todd and Greg followed Irene into the other room, while I stayed behind for a moment to calm myself. I wasn't going to be able to fall back asleep now, but this room was filled with books. If I was going to be awake, I might as well enjoy reading, and it might help me forget about the dead body in my parlor and the three unwelcome guests in the other room.

As I ran my finger along the bookcase, someone cleared their throat behind me. I froze, my heart sinking as I realized the night was far from over. Slowly, I turned around.

In the middle of the room, looking utterly bewildered and distinctly out of time, was a tall man with a full mustache, a formal waistcoat, and a wide-eyed expression of awe.

"Extraordinary," he murmured in a crisp British accent that belonged to another era. "Absolutely extraordinary."

My mouth fell open, and for a moment, no sound emerged. This was not happening. Not tonight. Not after everything else. For the past several weeks, I'd enjoyed a ghost free existence, something I hadn't experienced since the day I moved in. If I could make it to the stairs, up to my room, and under the covers, maybe he would go back to wherever he came from.

"There is an afterlife." His voice filled with wonder and what sounded suspiciously like vindication. "I knew it! I always suspected, but to experience it first-hand..." He paused, noticing me for the first time. "Your clothing is rather unusual, I must say."

I glanced down at the oversized t-shirt and leggings I wore for pajamas and realized how they must look to someone from his era. Odd, certainly, and possibly even scandalous.

He took several steps toward me. "You're not a spirit, are you."

I turned back to the bookcase and pretended I couldn't see or hear him.

"No, you're not." He came two steps closer. "But you can see me, can't you?"

"No," I said instinctively, the lie automatic after years of trying to hide my unwanted gift.

"Yes, you can!" he exclaimed with delight, clapping his hands together like an excited schoolboy. "You wouldn't have answered me otherwise. Unless you can't see me but only hear me? How fascinating! The mechanics of spiritual communication are far more complex than I ever imagined."

I tried for the door, but he stepped in my way, and I almost walked right into him. I'd learned that any physical contact with ghosts was an unpleasant experience, but he didn't seem to want to let me out the door without going through him.

"Why won't you speak with me?" he asked, as I did my best to dodge him.

"Stop that," I hissed. "I'm going back to bed, and you are absolutely not following me."

Greg poked his head into the study, his face pale in the candlelight. "Who are you talking to?"

"I'm talking to myself." I added a firm, "Good night," as I hurried past him and the ghost and ran up the stairs.

It was impossible to outrun a ghost, but I tried anyway. Shutting my bedroom door behind me, I jumped back into bed and pulled the covers over my head, hoping against hope that this new ghost hadn't learned he could walk through walls.

Fat chance.

"Finally!" The cultured British voice came from inside my room. "Someone who truly can see spirits. What a gift you have, what a wonderful, precious gift! I have so much to tell you, so many questions to ask, so much to share about the great beyond!"

"Go away," I said from under my comforter, my voice muffled by layers of cotton and down.

"My dear woman, this is absolutely thrilling! A genuine medium, a true sensitive! Do you know who I am?"

"No, and I don't care."

"I am Sir Arthur Ignatius Conan Doyle," he announced proudly.

CHAPTER 10

From where I hid under the covers, I imagined him giving a small, formal bow as he introduced himself.

"Go away," I said from under the covers where I planned to stay until he left.

"Surely, you've heard of me. I'm the author of many works of historical fiction, including *The White Company* and *Sir Nigel*."

If I stayed silent and perfectly still, maybe he'd think I'd fallen asleep and leave me alone. It was worth a try.

"Or perhaps you're more familiar with my spiritualist writings," he continued, his voice growing more animated. "My investigations into the supernatural, my communications with the spirit world. Or my historical novels about medieval England..."

His voice trailed off hopefully, waiting for some sign of recognition that I was determined not to give.

I poked my head out from under the covers, unable to contain myself any longer. "What are you talking about? No one has heard of any of those books or whatever you're going on about. You're famous for one thing and one thing only. Sherlock Holmes."

"Well, yes, I did write the Holmes stories, too," he said with what sounded like resignation. "And the Professor Challenger adventures, of course."

"Professor Who?" I asked before I remembered that I didn't care, and I told him so.

He stared at me for a long moment, his mustache drooping with what appeared to be profound disappointment. When he spoke again, his voice carried a mournful tone that tugged at something in my chest despite my irritation. "Is that all I'm remembered for? Only the Sherlock Holmes stories?"

I sat up in bed, pulling my knees to my chest and studying this dejected literary ghost. "Is that *all*? Listen, you've been dead for like a hundred years. Most people aren't remembered at all after that long. Their names and memories disappear like they never existed. I don't see why you're complaining about being immortalized as the creator of one of the most famous fictional characters ever written."

"More famous than Lord Peter Whimsey or Hercule Poirot?"

"Lord Peter who?" I wasn't about to get into a debate over Sherlock versus Poirot, and anyway, that wasn't the point. "If anyone has a right to complain, it's me. I was ghost-free for the first time since I moved into this house, and now you have to show up."

He peered at me curiously. "Tell me, my dear lady,

are you a medium? A clairvoyant? A natural sensitive? Have you had formal training in the spiritualist arts?"

"Listen, buddy," I snapped. "I'll ask the questions here. Like why are you still in my bedroom?"

He had the grace to look embarrassed, adjusting his cuffs with the careful precision of someone remembering proper etiquette. But instead of leaving, he settled into the corner chair near my window as if he planned to stay for quite a while.

"This must be fate," he said with growing excitement. "Destiny! A moment that was always meant to happen but has been far too long delayed."

"I'm going back to sleep," I announced firmly, falling back against my pillows and squeezing my eyes shut with the determination of someone who believed willpower could overcome supernatural persistence.

"But I've only arrived!" he protested, sounding wounded. "And there's so much to discuss! The nature of the afterlife, the mechanics of spiritual communication, the validation of everything I believed about the world beyond the veil!"

There was a soft tapping on my door, hesitant but persistent. Someone from downstairs, probably, wondering about all the commotion. If I ignored them, maybe they'd go away and leave me alone. If I was lucky, they'd take the ghost they'd summoned with them.

"April?" Jennifer's voice came through the door in a worried whisper. "Is everything alright? We heard voices."

Irma's more commanding tone followed immediately. "Who've you got in your room? Is it a man?"

I threw the covers aside, again, and went to unlock the door. Jennifer stood in the hallway wearing a pair of pink polka dot pajamas that made her look about twelve years old, while Irma wore...

"Bunnies?" I tried not to snicker, taking in the sight of my usually dignified friend in flannel pajamas covered with cartoon rabbits. "Thanks, I needed a laugh after the night I've been having."

"You've seen them before," Jennifer said defensively, though her cheeks pinked slightly.

"Yes, but on Irma they create a whole different effect," I said, unable to suppress a grin.

"What's going on?" Irma demanded, pushing her way into my room.

"Please, come on in," I said sarcastically as she looked around my room seemingly disappointed to find me alone. "I'll give you all the grisly details."

Jennifer wrinkled her nose before perching carefully on the foot of my bed. "I'd rather not hear anything grisly, thank you very much. I've had enough unpleasantness for one day."

"Don't worry, there's no blood and guts involved," I assured her. "Just a new ghost haunting me. Temporarily, I hope with all my heart. Irma, Jennifer, I'd like you to meet Sir Arthur Conan Doyle."

I gestured toward the corner chair where our distinguished ghost sat with perfect posture, looking like a Victorian gentleman caller who'd arrived at an inconvenient hour.

Jennifer gasped, her eyes widening as she looked in the direction I'd indicated but obviously seeing nothing. Irma squinted with the expression of someone trying to spot a rare bird that everyone else claimed to see.

Doyle rose from his chair and bowed deeply from the waist with the kind of formal courtesy that had gone out of style long ago. "Ladies, I am honored to make your acquaintance, even under these unusual circumstances. Can they see me too?" he asked hopefully, straightening his waistcoat.

"No, they can't see you," I said with a sigh. "Lucky me gets to have all the fun around here."

I told Jennifer and Irma about the midnight séance I'd come upon downstairs and the arrival of the new spirit.

"Where's he been all this time?" Irma asked. "Just floating around in the ether? I mean he's been dead for a long time, right?"

"Since 1930." Jennifer seemed happy to share one of the many facts she kept stored away in her brain. "He's been dead for more than ninety years."

Doyle's suddenly shaky voice broke into our conversation. "Ninety years? I don't suppose you happen to have any brandy? The shock of finding myself in the afterlife after nearly a century in limbo has left me rather rattled. I always found a good brandy settled my nerves."

"That's actually a great idea." I was thinking of my own nerves rather than his non-existent ones. "For me, anyway. You're a ghost, remember?"

"What's a great idea?" Jennifer asked, looking confused by my apparent non sequitur.

"Could one of you sneak downstairs and get me a brandy from the liquor cabinet? Maybe grab the whole bottle. I have a feeling our distinguished author here," I pointed toward the corner where Doyle was examining my bookshelf with interest, "isn't going to let me get any sleep tonight."

Irma tiptoed out of the room returning shortly with a snifter of brandy for me and one for herself. I encouraged both her and Jennifer to get some sleep.

"No reason for all three of us to be sleep-deprived tomorrow." I took a sip of the amber liquid and felt its warmth spread through my chest. "We're going to need our wits about us to deal with the living, the dead, and whatever else tomorrow decides to throw at us."

CHAPTER 11

After all the middle-of-the-night drama, I was wide awake. My mind buzzed with restless energy. Not that I could have slept since the ghost wouldn't stop talking.

"Murder?" Sir Arthur Conan Doyle's voice practically vibrated with excitement, like a child who'd been told Christmas was coming early. "You mentioned someone was murdered in this very house?"

"We think so," I rubbed my temples where a persistent headache had taken up permanent residence. The brandy had helped with my nerves but done nothing for the tension that seemed to be radiating from every muscle in my neck and shoulders. "She went up to the parlor to rest during the afternoon, and when we checked on her later, she was... gone."

"Tell me everything," he commanded, leaning forward in the corner chair with the intensity of a detective assigned to his first big case. "Every detail, no matter how insignificant it might seem. Leave nothing out." He settled back again, stretching his long legs out before him with the air of someone preparing for a weekend retreat devoted entirely to intellectual puzzles.

I sighed and stacked all my pillows against the headboard, arranging them into a comfortable nest. If I was going to be conducting a supernatural consultation at three in the morning, I might as well be comfortable. "Delilah, she's the one who died, was part of the Holmes Society. They booked my study for an afternoon tea fundraiser."

"The Holmes Society?" he interrupted. "As in Sherlock Holmes?"

"Yes, of course. Who else would it be?"

His mouth pursed as if he'd sucked on a lemon. "Not the 'Sir Arthur Conan Doyle Appreciation Society'? Or perhaps the 'Historical Fiction Enthusiasts'? The 'Spiritualist Research Group'?"

I gave him a look that could have frozen summer wine. "Would you like me to continue telling you about the murder, or shall we spend the rest of the night discussing your legacy?"

He had the grace to look slightly embarrassed. "Please, do go on. I apologize for the interruption."

"Delilah was the president of the organization," I continued. "She arrived dressed as Mrs. Hudson, though she clearly wasn't happy about the costume choice."

"Mrs. Hudson? Holmes' landlady?" Doyle stroked his magnificent mustache thoughtfully. "How peculiar.

One would think the president of the organization would choose a more... prominent role."

"That's exactly what I thought. According to what I overheard, she'd always played Irene Adler in previous events, you know, 'The Woman' from your stories. But this time, someone else had claimed that role."

"Ah, The Woman." His eyes lit up with the fond expression of a parent discussing a favorite child. "One of my finest creations, if I do say so myself. Brilliant, beautiful, and more than a match for Holmes himself."

"Yes, well, Greg, he's the vice president, showed up in full Sherlock Holmes regalia, complete with a deerstalker hat that looked like it had come straight from a BBC costume department. And the younger woman—"

"Younger?" Doyle interrupted again, his detective instincts apparently kicking in. "How old are these other players in our drama?"

I closed my eyes, trying to reconstruct the afternoon's events. "I'd say Delilah and Greg were both somewhere in their fifties or early sixties. Irene appeared to be around thirty, maybe early thirties. Young enough to be striking, old enough to know how to use her looks to get what she wanted."

"Interesting age dynamics," he mused, and I could practically see the wheels turning behind his eyes. "And this Irene. She was the one dressed as The Woman?"

"Exactly. And here's where it gets interesting. Irene had essentially taken over Delilah's role. You could feel the tension between them like electricity before a thunderstorm."

"Oh my." Doyle stroked his mustache again. "That is

quite fascinating. Wounded pride, usurped position, public humiliation, all excellent ingredients for murder. Do continue."

There was something oddly comforting about having someone to talk to about what had happened that day, even if that someone happened to be deceased. "Delilah bossed everyone around from the moment she arrived, including me. I did my best to smile and nod and not let her get to me."

"And how did the other's respond to her demands?"

"The others did what she told them to do, but you could see the resentment simmering beneath their politeness. Except for Rosalie." I paused, searching for the right word to describe the woman's behavior. "She was rather... what's the term I'm looking for? She smiled and acted as if she couldn't have been happier to be ordered around."

"Obsequious," Doyle suggested with the confidence of someone who'd spent a lifetime choosing precisely the right words.

I didn't have a dictionary in my bedroom, so I took his word for it. "She seemed so eager to please, almost painfully so."

"And who, exactly, is this Rosalie?" he asked, leaning forward with renewed interest. "Another member of our cast of suspects?"

"She and Todd round out our four potential murderers." I felt a pang of guilt for speaking so casually about people who were sleeping under my roof. But then I remembered that one of them might very well be a killer, and my sympathy evaporated. "Though

Rosalie left before we discovered Delilah's body. I wonder if she even knows what's happened. Maybe one of the others has managed to contact her somehow."

"Convenient departure," Doyle observed dryly. "And the two women who graced us with their presence a few minutes ago. Irma and Jennifer, was it? Are they also among our suspects?"

The suggestion was so absurd it made me snort. "Irma and Jennifer? Absolutely not. I've known them since I moved to town a few years ago. Irma has a heart of gold, and Jennifer is... well, she's about as dangerous as a butterfly in a rainstorm."

"My dear lady," Doyle said with the patient tone of someone explaining basic principles to a child, "in matters of murder, no one is above suspicion. The most unlikely person often proves to be the culprit."

I narrowed my eyes at him, feeling my protective instincts flare. "They are above suspicion, trust me on that. Neither of them had ever met Delilah before today. They're about as far from murder suspects as you can get."

"We shall see," he said with an infuriating know-it-all expression. "But for now, let us focus on our primary suspects. From your perspective, we have four individuals with potential motive and opportunity: Greg, Irene, Rosalie, and Todd. Is that correct?"

When I nodded, he continued with the methodical precision of someone who'd spent years coming up with complicated mystery plots. "Now, tell me about the victim's final hours. How did she behave? What did she consume?"

I took a deep breath and tried to organize my scattered memories of the afternoon. "Delilah seemed perfectly fine when she first arrived. She was full of energy and bossing around the other board members. And me and Jennifer. But when the event was ending, she seemed drained. She asked me if she could rest in another room," I continued, pulling the details from my tired mind. "I thought the event had worn her out. And then, when I noticed her slurring her words a bit, I thought she might have been drinking."

"And after death?" Doyle prompted gently.

"She looked so peaceful," I said, surprised by the catch in my voice. "Like she was asleep and having the most pleasant dream. If I hadn't known better, I would have thought she'd dozed off in my parlor."

"Gelsemium," Doyle said immediately, with the confidence of someone announcing the answer to a crossword puzzle he'd been working on for hours.

I blinked at him. "I'm sorry, what?"

"Gelsemium sempervirens," he repeated, clearly pleased with himself. "Mark my words, that's what killed the woman. Also known as yellow jasmine or Southern jessamine. Quite lovely to look at, potentially lethal to ingest."

He sounded so certain with his diagnosis, but it seemed like a huge leap from the little information I'd provided. "What makes you so sure? I mean, there are probably dozens of things that could cause similar symptoms, and not just poisons."

He puffed up like a peacock. "I conducted extensive experiments with gelsemium at one point in my medical career, and afterward, in my research for various stories. As I gradually increased my dose, I encountered the symptoms you describe. Initial alertness followed by gradual sedation, slurred speech, and loss of coordination. For those subject to a lethal dose, the result is a peaceful death that resembles natural sleep."

I narrowed my eyes. "Did you just casually admit to poisoning yourself? Because that seems like the kind of detail that should come with a warning label."

"In the name of science!" he declared, his chest swelling with righteous indignation. "A true researcher must be willing to suffer for knowledge, to push the boundaries of human understanding regardless of personal risk. How else can one write convincingly about such matters?"

The man had apparently been conducting dangerous experiments on himself which seemed questionable at best. "How old were you when you died? Because it seems to me that anyone willing to ingest plant toxins in the name of science, might not have had the longest life expectancy."

He waved away my concerns with a flourish of his ghostly hand. "I lived to the respectable age of seventy-one. But we're straying from the matter at hand. What haven't you told me about our suspects? Who among them had sufficient motive for murder?"

I nestled deeper into my carefully arranged pillows, feeling the full weight of exhaustion settling over me like a lead blanket. "That's the problem. None of them had obvious motive, or maybe all of them did, depending on how much Delilah had pushed them with her controlling behavior. Did I mention she was incredibly bossy? She'd made everyone around her feel like supporting players in her one-woman show."

I sat up suddenly as a detail surfaced from my exhausted brain. "I don't know if it's important, but Delilah had been romantically interested in Greg, but he seemed to be way more into Irene."

"Excellent!" Doyle rubbed his hands together with glee. "Love triangles and betrayal make the very best motives for murder. Though one might think such circumstances would make Delilah more likely to kill Irene, rather than the reverse."

"That's what I thought too," I agreed. "But maybe Irene saw Delilah as ongoing competition, someone who wouldn't give up. Or who might try to turn Greg against her. Eliminating the competition permanently would certainly solve that problem."

"Brilliant deduction," he said approvingly. "What about the others? Surely, there were other signs of tension or resentment."

I closed my eyes and had almost drifted off to sleep when I was jolted awake, by a clap of the hands.

My eyes popped open again. "What did you do that for?"

"You were about to tell me about the others."

"Right." The memory of hushed voices and overheard conversations came back to me. "There were lots of whispers. Greg might have been padding his expense account. And I'm not sure about the specifics, but Rosalie wasn't happy with Greg, and she didn't try that hard to hide it. Although, it's also possible that Rosalie was the one who was taking money from the club, and Greg was onto her."

The Holmes Society members had clearly brought more baggage to my tea party besides their elaborate costumes.

"And this Rosalie... She left early, you said?"

"She said she couldn't drive after dark, but honestly, it felt like an excuse." I shifted position again, trying to get comfortable, but not so comfortable that I fell asleep. "And then there's Todd, who had the most obvious crush on Rosalie I've seen since I was in high school. Either that, or they were already in some kind of secret relationship that they were trying to hide from the others."

Doyle nodded thoughtfully, apparently organizing all the information into some kind of logical framework in his ghostly mind. "A tangled web indeed. Financial impropriety, romantic jealousy, organizational politics, hidden relationships...We have quite the collection of classic motives."

"Oh." I'd almost left out the most intriguing clue. "I forgot to mention something that I have a feeling you're going to find very interesting."

"Yes?" He leaned closer and waited expectantly.

"Rosalie is an amateur herbalist."

"Dear lady, you just now thought to mention this?" His shoulders rose and fell as he sighed dramatically.

"This is no doubt the most important piece of information you have yet revealed. Do you not see that?"

"I suppose so, but I can't see Rosalie killing anyone. And besides, she gave the tonic to Irene, not Delilah."

"Tonic?" he asked. "What tonic?"

I explained that Rosalie had brought a small bottle of tonic for Irene along with some herbal tea blends and other gifts for the others.

"Can I go to sleep now?" I reached for my brandy snifter, disappointed to find it empty. "I'm running on fumes here, and tomorrow is going to be complicated enough without adding sleep deprivation to the mix."

"Sleep?" Doyle looked shocked by the suggestion. "With a crime to solve? A murderer to apprehend? My dear woman, how can anyone possibly think of sleep at a time like this? Especially when you have someone of my caliber available to assist you in unraveling this delightfully complex puzzle!"

I gave him the flattest look I could manage through my exhaustion. "You've been dead for almost a hundred years. I think the urgency of the situation might be a bit different from your perspective."

"Exactly!" he exclaimed, bouncing in his chair with enthusiasm. "I've had decades to hone my deductive skills, to observe human nature from the ultimate objective viewpoint. Death has freed me from the limitations of personal bias and emotional attachment. I'm at the very peak of my investigative powers!"

"That's great." I was already exhausted by him and his relentless energy.

"Imagine it," he continued, his eyes bright with possibility. "We could be the ultimate crime-solving partnership. The living and the dead working together to bring justice to the innocent and punishment to the guilty!"

"Like Holmes and Watson?" I asked dryly.

"Better than Holmes and Watson." He pulled an ornate pocket watch from his waistcoat, opened it with a flick of his thumb, and checked the time. "Better than any fictional detective. We are dealing with reality. Messy, complicated, gloriously unpredictable reality."

"Yay, reality," I grumbled.

He tucked the watch away, then stood abruptly. Pacing to the window and back with renewed energy, he waved his arms around as he spoke. "No time to waste on sleep when justice calls! We'll need to interrogate each suspect thoroughly, reconstruct the victim's final movements with scientific precision, examine every detail of the crime scene for clues that the authorities might have missed."

"The authorities haven't even arrived yet," I pointed out wearily. "The roads are still blocked from the earthquake damage, remember?"

"All the better! We'll have the advantage of a fresh crime scene, uncontaminated by well-meaning but ultimately inferior investigators." He turned to face me with the intensity of a general planning a crucial battle. "Tell me, was the victim served anything unusual during your tea service? Did she consume something that the others did not?"

"She drank the same tea as everyone else." I fought back a yawn. "Darjeeling, served from the same pot as everyone else at her table. And she ate the same food. I served finger sandwiches, mini quiches, scones with clotted cream and jam, and a selection of desserts. Maybe she had slightly larger portions than the others, but that's hardly unusual. I prepared everything myself, using ingredients I've used dozens of times before. And I confirmed that no one in attendance had any allergies."

"Hmm." His mustache twitched as though he were considering uncomfortable possibilities. "The delivery method must have been more targeted. Something added to her drink, perhaps. We'll need to examine the crime scene thoroughly, test any remaining food or beverages, interview each suspect about their movements during the crucial time period..." He stopped abruptly and turned to me with the expression of someone with a brilliant idea.

I had a feeling I wasn't going to like whatever he said next.

"Let's question them immediately, while their memories are fresh and their defenses are down. The guilty party will be least prepared to maintain their deception in the vulnerable hours before dawn."

"I'm sure they're all asleep by now." Although, if I were a murderer trapped in a house with limited escape routes, I'm not sure I'd be able to rest. "And speaking of sleep, if I don't get at least a few hours before morning, I won't be able to function."

He placed a dramatic hand over his ghostly heart. "Very well, my dear partner in detection. First thing in the morning, then. But I do hope you understand that every moment we delay gives our murderer additional time to cover their tracks, dispose of evidence, or plan their next move."

"Their next move?" I hadn't considered the possibility that Delilah's death might not be an isolated incident. "You think someone else might be in danger?"

"In my experience," Doyle said gravely, settling back into his chair, "murderers often don't stop with one victim, especially when they feel cornered or threatened. And nothing makes a killer feel more desperate than being trapped with others who know his or her darkest secrets."

With that unsettling thought, he walked through the door, leaving me at last alone in my room. I rearranged my pillows once more and closed my eyes, making a fervent wish that my dreams would be less bizarre than the previous twenty-four hours had been.

But as I finally began to drift toward sleep, with the weight of Arthur Conan Doyle's theories and the thought of a murderer in my house, I had the sinking feeling that things were only going to get stranger and more dangerous from here.

CHAPTER 12

The problem with ghosts, well, this one anyway, is that they never sleep. Sir Arthur Conan Doyle had been up all night, pacing the upstairs hallway like a restless professor waiting for his students to arrive. The old hardwood floors didn't creak under his ghostly feet, but I could feel his restless energy radiating through the walls of my bedroom like an electric current.

"At last, you have arisen," he said as I tiptoed past him trying not to wake the living inhabitants of my house. "There is no time to waste! The game is very much afoot!"

I held up a finger to my lips to quiet him before I remembered no one else could hear him. Greg snored loudly, his deerstalker hat abandoned on the floor beside his air mattress. Todd was still asleep on the sofa, one foot sticking out from under the blanket. His bright orange socks would have horrified any Victorian gentleman. Irene muttered sleepily and pulled her blanket over her head.

I crept into the kitchen, where the familiar and comforting scent of cinnamon rolls and freshly roasted coffee made my stomach grumble with anticipation. Everything seemed so normal, I could almost forget the events of the previous day and night. Jennifer and Irma were already bustling about, and I was about to take a seat at the island when something made me do a double take.

Irma was holding what appeared to be a small blow torch.

"What are you doing with that?" I asked, visions of my kitchen going up in flames dancing through my sleep-deprived mind.

"I found it in your pantry. I used to use one of these to caramelize the top of crème brülées at the Mermaid Café."

"That doesn't quite answer my question."

"I took the cinnamon rolls out of the freezer last night," Irma explained. "They're mostly thawed by now, but I thought they'd be even better if I warmed them up a bit in the microwave, and then I remembered. No power."

She flicked a switch, and a controlled flame appeared from one end of the little torch. I watched with fascination as she carefully waved it over the rolls until the cream cheese icing began to melt and bubble into golden perfection. I had to admit it was pretty clever, although I couldn't help thinking she could have wrapped them in foil and popped them in the gas oven.

Jennifer set a cup of coffee on the island in front of me. "Sorry, but no cappuccinos until the power comes back on. Luckily Irma found a family-sized French press in the pantry along with the blowtorch."

"You're an angel," I said gratefully, wrapping my hands around the warm mug and inhaling the rich aroma. "And possibly a mind reader. With Doyle talking all night long about clues and suspects and I don't know what else, I barely got a wink of sleep."

Sounds of stirring came from the living room, followed by Greg's groggy voice calling out, "Has anyone seen my deerstalker? Delilah will kill me if..." There was a long pause after which he muttered, "Never mind."

I filled a carafe with coffee, gathered three mugs, a sugar bowl, and a carton of creamer, and carried it all into the other room. In the morning light, the two men might have been actors who had fallen asleep on stage and awakened to find the play still going on around them.

"Coffee," Greg said as he walked over to the sidebar and filled a mug. "You're a lifesaver."

I lowered my voice. "Could you join me in the kitchen for a moment?"

"Is everything all right?" he asked.

"Yes, of course," I answered even though we both knew everything, from the closed road to the dead body upstairs, was not all right.

Irene, wearing a pair of Jennifer's pink polka dot pajamas, sat up rubbing her eyes. Greg's gaze flicked to her as she stretched and yawned, then he picked up his mug and followed me to the kitchen.

When Irma and Jennifer saw us enter, they exchanged meaningful glances, excused themselves, and went upstairs. Doyle leaned against the wall and observed Greg as we talked.

I pulled out a chair at the island for Greg and took a seat across from him. Anyone entering the room would think we were having a friendly chat over coffee instead of discussing someone's death.

"I wanted to ask you something," I said as casually as I could manage given the circumstances. "About gelsemium."

Greg's eyes widened with his coffee mug paused halfway to his lips. "You think that's what killed Delilah?"

"I didn't say that," I replied carefully, watching his face for any telltale signs of guilt or knowledge. "But you obviously know what it is."

He set down his mug and ran a hand through his disheveled hair. "Yes… vaguely. Most people in the Holmes Society know about it because Conan Doyle was fascinated by poisons and their effects."

Doyle stepped forward practically vibrating with excitement. "Obviously, the man is guilty! Note his immediate reaction. The widened eyes, the delayed response, the nervous gestures. And look there! Do you see that speck of yellow substance on his lapel? Where would one encounter gelsemium pollen at this time of year unless one had been handling the plant?"

I followed Doyle's pointing finger and noticed what

appeared to be a small yellow blob on Greg's wrinkled jacket. "You've got something on your lapel there." I gestured to the spot.

Greg looked down and his cheeks reddened with what appeared to be genuine embarrassment. "Oh, that. Yes, well, I have a confession to make. We got into your lemon curd last night after you went to bed. I have to say, it was delicious. I'll happily run to the store later and replace it if you'd like."

"That's not necessary." I filed away the information about their midnight kitchen raid. "I make the lemon curd myself, along with almost everything else we serve here."

"You do?" He grinned. "How did you manage to get that perfect balance of tart and sweet?"

"The secret is the lemons that come from the tree in the backyard," I explained, finding myself drawn into the familiar comfort of discussing cooking techniques. "There's nothing quite like freshly picked lemons for the sweetest juice. The fresher the fruit, the less sugar you need to balance the tartness."

Doyle was beside himself. "We are in the middle of a murder investigation, and you are sharing cooking tips with a suspect?"

"You know..." Greg leaned forward with renewed interest, "Conan Doyle wrote extensively about gelsemium. Is that what made you think of it as a possibility?"

"Yes, I couldn't sleep at all last night." I shot the ghost a glare, since he was the one who kept me up half the night. "So, I spent some time reading. I had printed out several articles about Sherlock Holmes and Sir Arthur Conan Doyle before your event. I always like to do at least some research when I'm hosting themed gatherings."

"That's very thorough of you," Greg said approvingly. He leaned forward and lowered his voice. "But since you're asking about gelsemium specifically, does that mean you don't think Delilah died from a heart attack or a stroke?"

"There's no way of knowing for sure until the coroner can get here," I said carefully. "Hopefully that will within the next few hours. Maybe when she arrives—"

"She?" Greg interrupted.

"Yes, Dr. Freddie Severs is our county coroner," I explained. "She's the best. Very thorough. I called her yesterday, and she promised me that as soon as the road crews clear the highway, she'll get here as soon as she can."

"That's a relief," Greg said, though he didn't look particularly relieved from where I was sitting. If anything, he appeared more anxious than before. "But if it wasn't natural causes, then that means..."

I nodded grimly. "It might be best if you don't say anything to the others. At least not until we know for sure."

He stared at his hands, seemingly lost in thought. "I guess that means we're all potential suspects. I mean, not you, of course."

"Probably not me," I agreed. "Or Jennifer or Irma,

since none of us had ever met Delilah before yesterday afternoon."

"Yes, of course, that makes perfect sense." He took a sip of his coffee, seeming to gather his thoughts. "But if you're looking for someone who might have had issues with Delilah, I hate to say it, but I'd probably start with Todd. He and Delilah had some kind of falling out recently over a podcast interview he was supposed to be recording today. I don't know all the details, so maybe it was nothing serious, but there was definitely tension there."

"Did everyone else get along well with Delilah?" I asked, though based on my observations yesterday, I was fairly certain the answer had to be no.

"Oh, absolutely," Greg said with a certainty that made me suspicious. "Everyone got along great. Delilah and Irene were really close, thick as thieves, those two. Always collaborating on ideas for special events and fundraising opportunities. Honestly, I think Delilah saw Irene as a kind of protégé, someone who could eventually take over some of her responsibilities."

I raised an eyebrow. "Close" was not how I would have described their relationship after the tension I'd witnessed between the two women.

"And Rosalie, of course, got along beautifully with everyone," he added casually, like he wasn't about to drop a bomb. "Did you know she's something of an amateur herbalist? Always mixing up homemade tinctures and tonics and whatnot. She knows quite a bit about plants and their properties."

He let this insinuation hang in the air, allowing me to draw my own conclusions.

"And you got along well with Delilah, too?" I asked. "I have to say, I did notice yesterday that she could be a little... bossy."

Greg waved a hand as if dismissing the very idea. "Delilah was always like that before an event. She wanted everything to be perfect. Better than perfect, if such a thing were possible. It was her way of showing how much she cared about the Society and its reputation. If you'd had the chance to meet her under different circumstances, you would have seen a completely different person. She truly had a heart of gold and was incredibly generous with both her time and her financial resources. We all benefitted from her generosity over the years."

"What a load of absolute hooey," Doyle said, forcing me to bite my lip to keep from laughing.

I gave Greg an understanding smile. "Thank you so much for putting my mind at ease. From what you've told me, I can see there's no way any of you could have had anything to do with Delilah's death."

"No way?" Doyle was practically shouting now. "My dear woman, have you taken leave of your senses entirely?"

"I'm so glad I could help clarify things." Greg stood, visibly relieved. "I'm always happy to serve in the pursuit of truth and justice. It's what Sherlock Holmes would have wanted."

As he left the kitchen with considerably more spring in his step than when he'd entered, Doyle fixed me with a look of profound disappointment. "Please tell me you don't actually believe a single word of that carefully constructed fiction."

"Of course not." I took another sip of my now lukewarm coffee. "You didn't see them all together yesterday afternoon. Delilah treated them like incompetent servants, and they did their best to hide how much they resented her, but I caught their expressions when they thought no one was watching. There was enough suppressed anger in that room to power the whole house."

"Ah, very clever." He nodded smugly. "Now that he thinks you believe him, he'll let his guard down. Perhaps you learned that technique from some of my stories. Often, Sherlock Holmes would allow suspects to think they had successfully deceived him."

"Exactly," I said, allowing him to take the credit. "Now we know that Greg is willing to throw Todd and Rosalie under the bus while making Irene seem as innocent as possible. What does that tell us?"

"That he's guilty!"

"Possibly. Or he's trying to cover for Irene. Or he wants to make himself seem beyond suspicion. The irony is, he did the opposite."

"I suppose you believe his convenient story about the lemon curd." Doyle didn't give me a chance to respond before launching into a monologue. "You clearly don't understand the critical importance of physical evidence, no matter how seemingly insignificant. A tiny speck of unusual substance, a missing shoe that later reappears in an unexpected location, a scratched lens on a pair of eyeglasses. In one of my most celebrated stories, 'The Adventure of the Second Stain,' a small ink smudge was the pivotal clue that allowed Holmes to unravel an entire conspiracy. Most people would have overlooked such a seemingly trivial detail."

Doyle continued his lecture while my mind sorted through Greg's half-truths and insinuations. If Delilah had been poisoned, and that was still a big "if," we still didn't know any details about how someone got it into her food or drink.

"It would help if we could figure out the motive," I said to Doyle when he finally paused for breath. "People don't kill people because they're annoying or bossy."

"Ah, but you'd be surprised how often seemingly minor irritations can grow into murderous rage," Doyle replied thoughtfully. "Pride, wounded dignity, thwarted ambition, romantic jealousy, financial desperation. The human heart is capable of remarkable darkness when pushed to its limits."

I nodded, considering our lineup of suspects. Like a perfectly baked shortbread, sooner or later, one of them was bound to crumble.

CHAPTER 13

It didn't seem right to keep all the cinnamon rolls to ourselves, especially when the smell of Irma's torchwork was probably drifting through the entire house and making everyone's mouths water. I set three rolls on plates, grabbed napkins, and headed into the front room to play hostess despite the circumstances.

Greg sat slumped in one of my armchairs with his nose buried in a leather-bound book that appeared to be a collection of Sherlock Holmes stories. Irene, still in pajamas, stood in front of my mahogany sideboard admiring what was left of my collection of vintage teacups, though I strongly suspected she was looking at herself in the mirror that hung above the display.

"I brought you something to tide you over," I announced, setting the plates down on the coffee table. "Where's Todd?"

"Being antisocial as usual." Irene gestured toward the front door.

I stepped onto the front porch, breathing in the cool, salt-tinged air. The wide porch was one of my favorite features of the old house, with its spectacular view of the ocean. Todd was slouched in one of the white wicker chairs, his legs stretched out before him and his gaze fixed on the distant horizon with the vacant expression of someone lost in thought.

The ocean was in a calm mood. Gentle waves rolled toward shore in steady, hypnotic rhythm, their white foam catching the morning light. A low mist clung to the tops of the shrubs along the path.

"Good morning," I said softly, not wanting to startle him from his contemplation.

He looked up with a slightly startled expression, as though he'd forgotten other people existed in the world beyond his own thoughts. When I handed him the plate, he took it with a grateful smile. "Thanks. That looks delicious."

I settled into the chair beside him, and we sat in silence for a few moments. The only sounds were the rhythmic crash of the waves and the caw of seagulls circling overhead. For a brief, precious interval, I could almost pretend we weren't trapped by earthquake damage with a dead body upstairs and three increasingly suspicious houseguests with possible motives for murder.

"Beautiful view," Todd said finally, his voice wistful. "You must love waking up to this every morning."

"You should come back and visit sometime when there isn't an earthquake. I mean not that you can predict those things, but chances are pretty good that if you came back for a normal weekend, there wouldn't be one." I became uncomfortably aware that I was rambling in the nervous way that always seemed to happen when I was trying to extract information from people. I decided to see if I could get him talking. "Sorry you didn't get to do your interview today. Is your podcast about Sherlock Holmes?"

"I did one episode about Holmes, but the show is about all kinds of mysteries, literary ones, historical puzzles, and real unsolved cases. There are fascinating mysteries all around us, hiding in plain sight if you know how to look for them. It might be a missing person case that the police gave up on, or an old local legend. Or even something as simple as a tree growing in a place where it has absolutely no business being. Everything has a story if you dig deep enough."

"Sounds like you'll never run out of ideas."

"I hope not." His tone was suddenly shy. "I've been asking myself what to do about this episode, this interview, since the moment I realized Delilah was dead. Maybe that should be the end of it."

"The end of what?"

"Sorry." He shook his head, staring down at the untouched cinnamon roll on his plate. "I'm not ready to talk about it yet."

"No need to apologize. Do you think you'll stay involved with the Holmes Society now that Delilah's gone?"

He answered with a noncommittal shrug.

"Let me ask that question a little differently." I

adopted a casual tone. "Will you stay in the group if Rosalie stays?"

His eyes flicked toward me. "Is it that obvious?"

"I've been told I'm pretty observant," I said with a gentle smile. "I noticed you two talking yesterday."

He hesitated, then nodded slowly. "Yeah. I… I like her. She's smart, thoughtful, and really sweet. But I don't know how she feels about me."

"That can be tough," I agreed. "A lot of people say you should be honest and tell the other person exactly how you feel, but what if they're not ready to hear it? Or what if it puts a strain on your friendship and ruins what you already have?"

"Exactly," he said with obvious relief. "It sounds like you're speaking from experience."

I let a few beats pass, enjoying the peaceful morning atmosphere, before I carefully introduced the topic I really needed to explore. "Do you think Rosalie would know anything about gelsemium?"

"If that's some kind of herb or plant, then probably. She says she's an amateur, but she's super knowledgeable. It's a passion for her." He paused, and I could see the exact moment when he put two and two together, his expression shifting. "Wait. Is that plant poisonous?"

"It can be, yes," I said carefully. "I was doing some reading about Arthur Conan Doyle last night. Apparently, he studied the effects of gelsemium and other poisons when he was doing research for his stories."

Todd frowned and shook his head. "Rosalie would never hurt anyone. She's turned over a new leaf, she…"

He stopped abruptly, clearly realizing he'd revealed more than he'd intended.

"Yes?" I prompted gently, hoping to encourage him to continue without seeming too eager or suspicious. "Was Rosalie in some sort of trouble in the past?"

"It had nothing to do with her plants or herbs or any of that stuff," he said quickly, his words tumbling over each other in his eagerness to defend her. "And no one was hurt." He reached out and placed a hand on my wrist. "Please don't say anything to anyone else about this. Please. I shouldn't have mentioned it at all."

"I don't know what I would say since you haven't really told me anything," I said lightly, standing and stretching like I wasn't cataloging his every word. "Enjoy the sea air and come back inside if you want another cup of coffee or anything else."

"Thanks for understanding," he said gratefully, his eyes already drifting back toward the sea. "Let me know if you find out when the road crews are going to get the highway cleared, okay?"

I stepped back inside and headed toward the kitchen, my thoughts churning like the waves outside as I processed this new information. Todd clearly had romantic feelings for Rosalie, that much was clear. But he'd also revealed enough to make me think that Rosalie might be hiding something more than her fondness for herbal tonics and natural remedies.

The question now was whether her past had any connection to the present, and whether whatever trouble she'd been involved in might have given her a reason to silence Delilah permanently.

CHAPTER 14

As I stepped back inside from the porch, the screen door settled behind me with its familiar creak. I left the heavy front door open to welcome the sea breeze, which always helped freshen the air throughout the house, especially when I'd been cooking all morning. Not that I planned to do much cooking today with my usual routines disrupted.

I heard Todd's voice drift in from the porch where I'd left him. "Rosalie. You came back."

Her answer came soft and hesitant. "Actually, I never really left. Are the others inside?"

A moment later, the screen door creaked open. Rosalie entered the room carrying a wicker basket with a red gingham cloth tucked around whatever treasures lay inside. Todd trailed behind her.

"These are for you from Sarah at the bed and breakfast." Rosalie held the basket toward me with both hands. "Fresh blueberry muffins she baked this morning. She thought you might be running low on baked goods with extra people to feed."

"That was so thoughtful." I took the basket and peeked inside at the enormous muffins which smelled heavenly. Sarah always baked far more than she or her guests could possibly eat.

Rosalie gave me a small, apologetic smile. "That's where I've been staying. The B&B, I mean. When I left here yesterday, I wasn't sure I'd make it all the way home before dark, and when I drove past the B&B, it was almost like the car stopped itself. It's such a gorgeous old house. Lucky for me, they happened to have a room available." She glanced around at the others, her expression seeking some kind of approval or forgiveness for her change of plans.

Todd, who'd been hovering close by, spoke up first. "I don't blame you at all for staying in town overnight. I was thinking I'd like to come back and spend a few days here later in the year. Hopefully when there's not an earthquake or power outage to deal with." He delivered the last part like it was meant to be a lighthearted joke, but I didn't think any of us was ready to find humor in our situation.

Greg stood. "Rosalie, do you... have you heard anything about Delilah?"

Rosalie blinked. "No, nothing. What about her?"

"She's gone," Greg said with the blunt delivery of someone who couldn't think of a gentler way to break terrible news.

"She left?" Rosalie's brow furrowed as she tried to

make sense of this information. "But the road is still blocked, isn't it? How could she have gotten out?"

"I mean she passed away," Greg clarified, his voice heavy with the weight of having to repeat this information. "She died yesterday afternoon."

Rosalie's hand flew to her mouth. "Oh no. No, that can't possibly be true. Not Delilah."

"It is true, I'm afraid," Greg continued with grim certainty. "She went upstairs to lie down after the event, before the earthquake hit, and when we went to check on her later that evening..."

"I was the one who found her," Irene interrupted. "It was awful. Although she looked so peaceful lying there that I had no idea that she was dead at first. I thought she was asleep, but she wouldn't wake up."

Rosalie reached out with one hand as though searching for something solid to steady herself against. Todd stepped forward and took her arm, guiding her to the nearest chair. She began to cry as we all stood around helplessly.

"Can I get you anything?" I asked finally, feeling helpless as she sobbed. "Coffee? A glass of water?"

She lifted her head and wiped tears from her cheek with her sleeve, staring at me as if she didn't understand the question.

"I'll get you a cup of tea." Still holding Sarah's basket of muffins, I retreated toward the kitchen.

Doyle was waiting for me in the kitchen with the patient attention of someone who'd been observing everything.

"She's the one," he announced without any preamble, his tone carrying absolute conviction.

I set the basket down on the counter and put the kettle on before turning to him with raised eyebrows. "Excuse me?"

"Rosalie," he said with the satisfaction of someone who'd solved a challenging puzzle. "I'm quite certain she's the one who poisoned Delilah."

I reached for my favorite teapot and began scooping my special tea blend into the infuser while I waited for him to explain his reasoning. "Would you care to share how you came up with that conclusion?"

"There is, of course, her obvious expertise in herbal remedies and botanical preparations, but there are additional clues that point to her guilt," he said with the methodical precision of someone presenting evidence. "There's a distinct smell of mint about her person. I have deduced she is attempting to disguise the scent of alcohol on her breath with peppermint pastilles or some similar breath freshener." He paused for dramatic effect, then delivered his final assessment with grave certainty. "She is consuming alcohol to numb her overwhelming feelings of guilt after murdering her friend."

"Right." I poured hot water over the tea leaves and tried to ignore the tight knot that was forming in my stomach. "Or maybe she brushed her teeth this morning. These days, people use minty toothpaste as part of their daily hygiene routine. Maybe people didn't have that luxury in your era."

"Of course we brushed our teeth," he replied with

obvious offense at the suggestion that his dental hygiene had been neglected.

"What I want to know is why she brought a change of clothes when she supposedly hadn't planned to spend the night in town."

"Yes, that's precisely what I was about to mention."

"Of course you were," I murmured, setting the teapot, cups, sugar bowl, and cream pitcher on a tray.

I carried the tea into the front room. Todd hovered near Rosalie, who had stopped crying but seemed to be in shock. Greg paced restlessly near the windows.

"Here we are." I set everything down on the coffee table. "My favorite tea blend. It's a blend of Chinese black tea, Keemun, and red rose petals. I find the aroma calming, but if anyone would rather have coffee, I can make another pot." I remembered the basket still in the kitchen. "I completely forgot the muffins that Rosalie brought us from Sarah's. You probably think I'm hoarding them all for myself."

Rosalie stood. "I'll come with you to get them." She followed me back into the kitchen, but instead of taking the basket of baked goods back to the others, she lingered, watching me make a fresh pot of coffee.

"Good thing you brought a change of clothes," I said breezily. "I bet the others are wishing they'd thought to pack an overnight bag."

She froze for the tiniest fraction of a moment before saying, "Yes, I always bring a bag when we're doing special events, especially when they're this far from home. I'd feel a little embarrassed stopping at a restaurant dressed in costume."

Jennifer's footsteps and voice preceded her appearance on the back stairs. "You might be surprised how well people respond to period costumes. They're real conversation starters." She swept past us. "Oh, Muffins! Can we have some?"

"Yes." I waved at the basket. "Sarah sent over at least a dozen."

"Yum." She grabbed two. "I talked Irma into watching *Pride and Prejudice*. She's never seen it. Can you believe it?"

"The movie or the miniseries?" Rosalie asked.

Jennifer scoffed. "The miniseries. Young Colin Firth is to die for." She skipped back up the stairs leaving Rosalie and me alone again, if you didn't count Doyle. He was hard for me to ignore as he stood mere inches from her, examining every fiber of her clothing with the intensity of someone conducting a forensic investigation.

I could sense that Rosalie wanted to talk, so I offered her a cup of coffee, which she accepted.

As she added a teaspoon of sugar, she asked, "How did Delilah really die?"

I kept my voice even. "I was told she had heart problems."

"But it's so sudden." Rosalie took a sip of her coffee then set the mug down. "And she was on medication for cholesterol and high blood pressure. Maybe she'd forgotten to take her pills, but that wasn't like her."

I shrugged lightly. "Why do you think it might be something else?"

Her eyes met mine briefly, then she focused on the

basket of muffins. She selected one and began peeling back the paper wrapper slowly, almost meditatively, before she finally spoke. "Because someone wanted her dead."

There it was. That small, deliberate truth dropped into the room like a pebble in a still pond.

And I had the distinct feeling there were more ripples to come.

CHAPTER 15

I stared at her, caught off guard by her words and stunned that she'd decided to share them with me. "Someone wanted Delilah dead? Who?"

Rosalie held her mug cupped in both hands. "Take your pick. You met the woman. Don't tell me you weren't about ready to strangle her yourself after spending one afternoon in her company."

"I'll admit she tested my patience, but if people were murdered because they were obnoxious or difficult, there would be a lot fewer people in the world."

She picked at her muffin like she'd lost her appetite but wanted to be polite. "Sarah's a wonderful baker."

I refilled my teacup. "I'm surprised she had a room available for you at the last minute. She's been booked solid since the hotel closed for renovations, especially on the weekend."

"I guess I got lucky and someone cancelled." She took another bite of the muffin, chewing like someone who wanted to keep their mouth full a little longer than necessary.

"That was lucky," I agreed, letting silence settle for a beat. "I wanted to thank you again for the herbal teas you gave us. How did you learn so much about plants and herbs?"

Rosalie brightened. "My grandmother. She kept a garden full of things most people called weeds. She always said every plant had its use, as long as you knew what it was trying to tell you. I started helping her when I was maybe six or seven, cutting leaves, drying flowers, making salves and teas. She had the most amazing garden. When I was little, I thought fairies must live there among all those wonderful plants."

"That sounds magical." I smiled, stirring my tea though I hadn't added anything to it. "I went down a rabbit hole learning about herbs when I was researching for your event. Sir Arthur Conan Doyle was surprisingly knowledgeable on the subject."

Rosalie looked amused. "Let me guess what you discovered. Belladonna, wolfsbane, mandrake..."

"And gelsemium." I casually watched her face for any telltale reaction.

She blinked once, a slow deliberate blink. "That's not one you hear people talking about every day."

"I'm sure you know that Doyle wrote a paper on its effects," I continued in the tone of someone sharing an interesting historical tidbit. "He thought it could be used medicinally in small doses for neuralgia, asthma, things like that."

"That's true," Rosalie said. "But in larger amounts, it's deadly. Not the kind of thing you leave lying about."

I gave a little laugh. "No, definitely not. But fascinating, right? The line between remedy and poison is thin."

"Very thin," she said softly. "I get the feeling you think that Delilah was poisoned."

"It's a possibility. Until the coroner can reach us and examine her properly, we won't know for sure what caused her death."

Rosalie's posture stiffened. "I hope you're not trying to imply that I had anything to do with her death."

Doyle took an eager step closer. "That's exactly what we're implying!"

"No, of course not." I sipped my tea to hide how uncomfortable I felt even hinting that she could have committed murder.

Doyle leaned over her shoulder like a professor who suspected his student of cheating on a test. "She's dodging like the guilty character in *The Adventure of the Speckled Band!* I knew it from the moment she walked through that door. She's absolutely our culprit."

I did my best to ignore his enthusiastic commentary, instead gesturing toward the remaining muffins. "Would you mind taking those out to the others before they think we're holding out on them?"

Rosalie picked up both the plate and her mug, but she hesitated at the kitchen door as though she had more to say before returning to the others. But if she did, I never found out what it was.

As the door swung shut behind her, Doyle puffed up. "She's hiding something."

"Definitely," I said. "But does it have anything to do with Delilah's murder?"

The kitchen door creaked open again, and Irene leaned her head through the gap. Jennifer must have loaned her an outfit, since she'd changed from pajamas into a red polka-dot shirt and capris pants.

"I thought I heard you talking to someone in here." She held out a teapot with both hands. "I came to ask if I could get some more hot water."

I took the china pot from her and set it on the counter while I put the kettle back on the stove to boil. "I can make some herbal tea if everyone's had enough caffeine for one morning. I was thinking of trying one of Rosalie's blends."

She wrinkled her nose. "Yes, that would be nice, but I'd love more of your rose petal tea. It was really good."

"You're not a fan of her teas, then?" As I grabbed the tea cannister, I did my best to sound casual. "I heard she gave you a tonic she made."

"She put it in the cutest little bottle." She lowered her voice. "Can I make a confession?"

Doyle practically leapt to attention. "This is it. I knew she was the killer. I knew it all along."

"What is it?" I asked expectantly.

"I don't like the tonic at all," she admitted with obvious relief at finally being able to speak the truth. "It tastes disgusting. I poured it down the bathroom sink."

Doyle's shoulders slumped. "That's her confession? She's a wastrel?"

"But if you don't like it, why did you tell her you did?" I asked. "Everyone said you loved it, and she made it especially for you. And why would you pour it down the drain?"

Irene sighed and settled herself on one of the kitchen stools. "I couldn't bring myself to tell her the truth, not after I'd said how much I liked it that first time. I was being polite. I didn't expect her to keep giving me bottles of it every single time we got together. You know how people are with their 'special' homemade creations. It's like that one dish someone's grandmother insists on bringing to every potluck dinner. Nobody wants to be mean, but no one wants to eat it either. But I love the little vintage bottles she puts it in, so I dump out the tonic and keep the bottles."

Doyle perked up again. "Tell me that isn't suspicious! She deliberately disposed of potential evidence!"

I had another question for Irene. "Before you tossed it out, did you share it with anyone? Like, Delilah maybe?"

"Why do you ask? Do you think...?" She paused, tapping her chin with her index finger. "I heard that Delilah took medication for her heart. Everyone says that herbal remedies and prescription meds can be bad to take together." After a moment she seemed to shrug off the idea. "But if she had some of Rosalie's tonic, she didn't get it from me."

"And I don't suppose you know who might have

access to gelsemium?" I asked, watching her face for any sign of recognition.

"I really wouldn't know about that," she said. "That sounds like a question for Rosalie." She lowered her voice. "You're not suggesting that Rosalie had anything to do with Delilah's death, I hope."

"Of course not." I assured her with what I hoped was a convincing smile, then decided to test a different theory. "I haven't read many of the Sherlock Holmes books, but ever since your group booked your event, I've been becoming more interested. Who's your favorite character?"

"Irene Adler," she said immediately. "I mean, she's iconic."

"Yes. The Woman. What story would you recommend I read next?"

"If you haven't read *The Hound of the Baskervilles* yet, you should read that one."

"Yes, I like stories about dogs." I paused to see if she'd take the bait, but her smile didn't falter. I added a worm to the hook. "The Basset Hound in the story sounded so cute with his long floppy ears and droopy jowls."

"Oh, yes." Irene agreed. "They're the cutest."

Doyle groaned. "Basset Hounds? The hound in my story is a supernatural hell hound, not a cuddly puppy."

While Doyle ranted, I somehow managed to maintain my pleasant expression while Irene beamed, totally unaware of her blunder. I refilled the teapot and handed it to her.

"May I have another muffin?" she asked.

Handing her the basket, I said "Take as many as you like."

Doyle called after her retreating form, "You're a fraud!"

"She can't hear you, you know," I reminded him once the door had closed behind her.

"Who can't hear who?" Irma stood at the second to the bottom stair looking around the room. "Talking to Sir Arthur I suppose."

"Sure am."

Doyle turned to me, all indignation. "That girl knows nothing about my stories! I'm telling you, she's our murderess."

"You said the same thing about Rosalie not twenty minutes ago," I pointed out. "And by the way, these days we don't refer to adult women as girls."

He ignored both of my comments. "Did you observe how innocent and naïve she did her best to appear? That might fool some people, but not me."

Irma seemed entertained by my half of our conversation, settling herself comfortably at the island to listen.

"We're talking about Irene," I told Irma, then turned back to Doyle. "I'm not entirely sure it's an act. I don't know how innocent she is, but she's certainly not particularly worldly or sophisticated. Did you notice the way she seemed to want to implicate Rosalie while at the same time defending her?"

Irma grabbed a muffin from the basket then gave me a sly smile. "I waited at the top of the stairs for the two of you to finish talking so I didn't interrupt you. It was almost like she couldn't decide whether she wanted us to think her friend was guilty or innocent. What does your ghost buddy the famous author have to say about all this?"

"Irene is guilty," Doyle and I said in perfect unison.

"Though before that, he was convinced Rosalie was the guilty one," I added.

"I assume he has better reasons for suspecting Irene than thinking women are cunning and untrustworthy," Irma said with the dry tone of someone who'd dealt with masculine prejudices her entire life.

"Also, they lie. But in this case, he's right, at least about Irene and Rosalie. Neither of them is telling the whole truth. What I want to know is why they're lying."

CHAPTER 16

Hoping for some news, I pressed the power button just long enough for the screen to flicker to life. One wavering bar of service. But it was enough to find out that there was no real news, at least not a firm estimate about when we could expect the power to be restored or the road to be cleared. There was no word from Freddie or Andy, but they'd probably stayed up all night helping in whatever way they could.

I was about to turn the phone off again when it buzzed with a text from Freddie.

Crew will clear the road today. As soon as I can, I'll be there. Stay safe.

I sighed and sent her a quick thanks, then powered the phone back down. No news wasn't exactly good news, but at least it wasn't worse.

The body was still upstairs. The murder suspects were still trapped with us. And Sir Arthur Conan Doyle's ghost had taken up semi-permanent residence.

"No news?" Irma asked.

"You could tell by the look on my face, huh?"

Jennifer's footsteps came down the stairs, thudding softly on each one. "Oh, there you are," she said to Irma. "I thought you were coming back."

Irma gave an exaggerated huff. "I don't get *Pride and Prejudice*. What kind of ending was that? It didn't even seem like it ended."

Jennifer looked about as annoyed as I'd ever seen her. "That's because it wasn't the end. It was just the first episode."

"Oh. That makes more sense." She nudged me with her elbow. "I'm bored. Got anything I can clean?"

Jennifer put her hands on her hips. "You'd rather clean than watch a show with me?" She made an about face and clomped back up the stairs.

Trying hard not to laugh, I asked Irma if she was serious about cleaning.

"Sure. It helps me relax."

"You could try meditation," I suggested.

Irma waved that off. "Naw. I need to do something. Why don't I clean the downstairs bathroom?"

"Not until after our guests leave. I never finished cleaning the study after the event. You could help me…"

I didn't even finish the sentence before Irma was rummaging around under my sink, pulling out gloves and a sad looking sponge that should have gone into the trash long ago. I went into the back room and returned with a caddy stocked with cleaning supplies and two bussing bins, one for her and one for me.

"Perfect." She grabbed another candle from the shelf and lit it. "Let's bring some light and Lemon Pledge to the scene of the grime."

Our four guests looked up when we emerged from the kitchen. I pointed towards the study. "We'll be in there if you need us."

The heavy velvet curtains in the study blocked what little light filtered through the overcast sky. The air smelled faintly of dust and old paper. I pulled the curtains aside, letting in a thin wash of pale light, then lit the tea candles sitting on the tables. Between the flickering candles and the scent of old books and rosewood furniture polish, the room was the perfect spot for a séance.

Apparently, Greg had thought so too.

Doyle wandered the room, his fingers trailing over spines of books, stopping every so often to take a closer look at a title or a faded photograph.

Meanwhile Irma got to work, filling her bin with plates and silverware. I carried several tiered trays to the kitchen and returned to find Doyle staring at one of the water glasses on the center table where the society members had sat.

"Small details," Doyle said, as though he'd been waiting for an audience to share his wisdom. "Always the small details that lead to truth. For example—"

I whispered to Irma, "The esteemed author is regaling me with his crime-solving expertise."

He huffed but kept talking. "As I was saying, small details such as the lipstick on this glass can crack a case." He pointed at one of the water goblets.

Intrigued, I made my way to the table. The glass had a perfect impression of a lower lip in bright red lipstick.

"Delilah," I murmured. "She's gone, but her lipstick stays behind."

Irma glanced over. "A good scrub will get rid of that."

Doyle perused the bookshelves and continued talking about not overlooking small details, rambling about a Sherlock Holmes story I'd never even heard of.

I wasn't listening. I was looking at Delilah's teacup. "Not even a hint," I murmured.

"What's that?" Irma asked.

"Nothing." The teacup at Rosalie's seat had a smudge of pink. So did her water glass. There weren't any lipstick smudges on Irene's glass or teacup, but that's what I would have expected. She probably wore nothing more than lip gloss.

Irma picked up the bin full of dishes and braced it against her hip. "You okay?"

"Sure." I didn't take my eyes off Delilah's glass and the lipstick mark. "Let's leave this table as is, okay? I'll cover it in a sheet. I'll tell everyone it's off limits, say it's on order of the sheriff."

Doyle abandoned the books and came to stand next to me. "Have you found a clue?" When I pointed at the glass, he said, "The lipstick. I knew it!"

"You did?"

"If you recall, I mentioned the lipstick when you first came into the room."

"Yes. You forgot to point out that the glass has red lipstick on the rim, and the teacup doesn't."

He took a closer look. "I noticed that immediately, didn't you? Do I have to point out every single clue and explain to you the relevance of said clue?"

"It would be helpful."

I opened one of the cupboards where I kept white sheets specifically for draping over tables. That allowed us to set the tables a day or more in advance and not worry about them getting dusty. Irma helped me drape it gently over the table.

"Aha!" Doyle exclaimed, pointing dramatically to the rug beneath the chair.

"Excuse me?" This was my own fault for insisting he tell me about every tiny possible clue he found.

I leaned over, and sure enough, there was a small, round button. Charcoal gray, plastic, with two holes. I stared at it, feeling like I should know where it came from.

"Now what?" Irma asked as I crouched down. "Don't tell me we've got bugs. That would add a special touch to this weekend."

"No bugs." I took a clean teaspoon and picked up the button, holding it out to show Irma.

She stared at it, then looked up at me. "Okay, the lipstick I get. Sort of. But a button?"

I shrugged. "You never know."

Jennifer entered the room. "What have you got there?" She came closer, grinned, and snatched the button from me. "I've been looking for that everywhere. Thanks!"

I looked over at Doyle, but he was pretending to ignore me. "Thank Sir Arthur Conan Doyle. No case is too small for him."

"Um, thanks." She noticed the shrouded table. "Why is there a tablecloth draped over the table?"

I lifted one side of the sheet and pointed to Delilah's place setting, explaining that it didn't appear that she'd drunk from that particular teacup.

"I saw her drinking tea." She leaned closer. "Too bad Delilah insisted that all the teacups match, or we might be able to tell if someone had switched them. Do any of the others have a red stain?"

"They don't. I'm not sure if it means anything, but until we know for sure what killed Delilah, we have to consider the possibility that she was poisoned. Which is why," I said quietly, "I think we should leave everything exactly where it is. Just in case. No one else comes in here, okay? Not until Freddie or the sheriff gets here."

Jennifer nodded. "Got it. The room is officially off-limits."

"I'll put up a sign," Irma said. "How about 'Crime Scene: Do Not Enter'?"

"Maybe something a little less dramatic," I said. "Like locking the door?"

Before I did that, I took one last look at the room. Something about the whole setup still prickled at the edge of my thoughts.

Doyle was right. The answers were here, in the details. I just had to figure out how they fit together before the road opened and the four suspects were someone else's problem.

What was so wrong with that? Nothing really, except for the high probability that one of them would get away with murder.

CHAPTER 17

Everyone was gathered in the front room like characters in the last ten minutes of an Agatha Christie adaptation—slightly stir-crazy, overly suspicious, and deeply disappointed that the police hadn't shown up yet to point fingers and pronounce justice.

Jennifer came down the stairs holding a board game in her arms and a hopeful sparkle in her eye. "Anyone want to play Clue?"

Greg grunted. "That game's for kids."

Irene, perched elegantly on the settee, sighed. "Only if I can be Miss Scarlet."

"I'm always Miss Scarlet," Jennifer said under her breath.

"I don't mind being Colonel Mustard," Todd said cheerfully. "Tell me something. If there's a Colonel Mustard, why isn't there a Major Mayonnaise?"

Greg groaned at the joke, but the others played along.

"Or Private Pickle," Irene suggested.

Todd laughed, then came up with, "Lieutenant Lettuce."

Irma, who had slipped from the room, returned waving a deck of cards. "I vote poker. Winner gets this chocolate bar I found in the pantry." She set the candy on the coffee table like she was placing a huge bet.

Within seconds, Jennifer's game was abandoned on the floor as everyone converged on the table like moths to an electric lantern.

I couldn't blame them. A game of Clue probably hit a little too close to home at the moment.

Jennifer sat back, arms crossed, visibly disappointed. I caught her eye and gave her a small shrug of sympathy, but there wasn't much else I could offer.

The one battery-operated clock told me it was past noon, which meant I should probably feed my stranded guests. "How about sandwiches?"

Everyone answered with enthusiasm, so I retreated to the kitchen, where I could think and bounce ideas off my latest ghost. It reminded me of the long conversations I'd have with Chef Emile, although most of the time they were one-sided, with him criticizing my cooking techniques. Still, the memory made me smile.

Doyle hovered by the cappuccino machine. "How are you possibly thinking about food when there's a murder to solve?"

"I'm trying to keep everyone from reenacting *And Then There Were None*. You know, the Agatha Christie story where everyone is murdered."

"Of course I know. A brilliant author, but her plots

were at times shall we say…convoluted? And yet, somehow, predictable."

I sensed some professional jealousy. "Unlike your stories, I'm sure."

As I assembled sandwiches from what I could find in the refrigerator and the pantry, he droned on about the praise heaped on him for his stories. "One of the reviews said, 'No one could have expected that ending.'"

I interrupted his self-praise. "Tell me more about the symptoms of gelsemium poisoning."

"Ah, so you're finally coming around to my way of thinking," he said with a smug look. "It depends on the dosage, but let's assume it's a rather large dose meant to be fatal. There would be muscle weakness. Dizziness. Blurred vision. Labored breathing. And if enough is ingested, there will be paralysis of the respiratory system. In other words, one stops breathing. It's quick, but not always immediate."

I paused halfway through slicing a tomato, the knife still in my hand. A faint chill traced its way up my spine.

"When Delilah asked if she could rest somewhere, she told me she felt tired and…" I tried to remember her exact words. "Woozy. And she was slurring her words. Honestly, I thought she was a little tipsy. I found out later she doesn't, or rather didn't drink at all."

Doyle nodded sagely. "Classic presentation. And, if I may add, your suspect list remains robust."

I was about to ask him to elaborate when Irene appeared in the doorway, looking pale but perky.

"Oh, hello," she said. "It's really nice of you to make us lunch considering you're kind of stuck with us."

"It's easier than making afternoon tea for a room full of people. Want to keep me company while I work?"

"I'd be happy to. Anything I can do?"

"Just chat." I set out slices of sourdough and arranged tomato slices, cucumber rounds, and cheese on a plate.

"Sounds great." She pulled up a stool. "Anything in particular you want to chat about?"

Doyle spoke up. "Yes. Why you killed Delilah!"

It wasn't easy to tune out the ghost, but I did my best. "I'd love to see the little bottle Rosalie's tonic came in. I'm thinking of bottling lavender simple syrup as gifts, and I've been looking for cute little bottles to put it in."

I watched her face carefully as I spoke. A beat too long passed before her answer.

"I threw it away."

"You threw it away? But I thought you said you poured out the tonic and kept the bottle."

"No." She smiled tentatively. "I threw away the bottle."

"In one of the trash cans in the house?"

Her smile faltered. "No… I don't remember."

"Irene…" I gave her a look usually reserved for unruly children.

She hesitated. "Fine. I didn't pour it out."

"Aha!" Doyle stood next to Irene, his nose mere inches from hers. "Why did you lie?"

Giving him a quick glare, I asked in a gentle tone of voice, "Did you give some to Delilah?"

She swallowed hard. "She had a headache, and I thought the tonic might help. I didn't see how it could hurt and anyway, if she is on medication, then it's up to her to know if something might interact or whatever."

I kept my voice even, which wasn't easy. "Why didn't you tell me that before?"

"She's hiding something," Doyle ranted. "Isn't it obvious?"

She twisted a strand of hair around her fingers. "I didn't want to get Rosalie in trouble. She makes that stuff with all kinds of ingredients, and sometimes I'm not sure they're even legal. I figured if Delilah had an allergy or a reaction or something, it was her own fault. I didn't make her drink it."

My mind whirled as I put the pieces together. "Irene, if there was poison in that bottle, I'm almost sure it wasn't meant for Delilah."

She blinked. "What are you saying?"

"I'm saying that if someone tampered with the tonic, it might have been intended for you. Think about it. You were the one who was supposed to drink it."

For once, she didn't have anything to say. At least, not right away.

"No," she whispered. "Rosalie would never hurt me."

"It wasn't necessarily Rosalie. Someone else could have put something in the tonic either before or after she gave it to you. Is there anyone in the group who might want to… hurt you?"

Irene bit her lip. "Not Greg." She paused. "And not Rosalie."

That left Todd.

Her eyes flicked toward the dining room, where a burst of laughter signaled someone had won a hand of poker. Likely Irma. The cheerful sound seemed to echo with a darker undertone now, as though the house itself were reminding me how thin the line between laughter and danger could be.

Doyle gave a low whistle from across the room. "I believe I mentioned that every story has a twist."

I shushed him with a flick of my hand and passed Irene a turkey sandwich.

"Eat," I said gently. "You'll feel better."

I wasn't so sure I would. Because if Irene was telling the truth, then someone was playing a dangerous game. One with deadly consequences.

CHAPTER 18

Irene stared at her sandwich while I made more, lining them up neatly on platters.

"I'll need the tonic," I said.

"Why?"

"For safekeeping. And to get it tested later."

She finally took a bite of her sandwich and chewed slowly, clearly buying time. Finally, she whispered, "You think it has poison in it?"

"I don't know. I just need to make sure no one else has access to it." Although, even if I had possession of Irene's bottle of tonic, that didn't mean there wasn't another. Or someone might have a supply of gelsemium that they could add to anyone's food or drink.

That was a chilling thought.

Irene took another bite of her sandwich, but didn't make a move to get the tonic.

"Irene." My voice was firm and impatient. I didn't

have the time or inclination to baby her. "Hand over the tonic now."

She stood, and with a reluctant sigh, reached into her pants pocket and pulled out the decorative glass bottle with its lacy ribbon still tied around the neck. I held out my hand and she set it in my palm. It was much smaller than I'd expected, about three inches high.

"I'll guard it with my life." I slipped it carefully into my pocket.

Irene and I carried the platters of sandwiches into the other room where Irma was having the time of her life. She barely looked up, apparently too busy winning everyone's spare change.

Jennifer jumped up from her seat when she saw Irene and me carry in the food. She got plates and napkins for everyone, then followed me back to the kitchen to help with drinks. When she looked in the freezer, she sighed.

"The ice is melted." She closed the freezer door. "I guess it's going to be lukewarm tea instead of iced tea."

"Should I even bother making lemonade?" Warm lemonade didn't sound refreshing to me.

Jennifer ducked into the pantry and returned with a bottle of pink liquid. "We have a whole case of hibiscus coolers back here, and they're not warm at all."

"I'd rather save those for paying guests, but we'll see how the day goes."

We carried a pitcher of water and another of room-temperature tea and set them on the sideboard just as

Todd lay his cards face down and stood. "That's all the cash I have on me."

"I take debit cards," Irma said, and I wondered if she was serious. I never knew with her.

"I think I'll drive back over and check on the road closure. Maybe we can get an update. It would be nice to get home by tonight and sleep in my own bed. Anyone want to come with?" He looked hopefully at Rosalie who didn't seem to be paying attention.

"I'll go along." Greg stood and headed for the front door. "I'm getting cabin fever sitting around here."

The two men left, and I picked up the empty plates and trash. Irma turned to Irene. "Care for a game of Texas Hold 'em?"

"Or Clue?" Jennifer asked with a shy smile.

"I'd love to play Clue," Irene said. "Can I be Miss Scarlet?"

"And can I hit her over her head with a wrench in the conservatory?" Irma mumbled just loud enough for me to hear her.

I was happy to see Rosalie didn't seem to be interested in the game since I wanted to talk with her some more. "Would you like to see our secret garden?"

"It's not really a secret," Irma said. "I don't know why she calls it that."

I chuckled. She knew exactly why I called it that, but it had become her favorite joke.

"We'll wait to start playing until you get back," Jennifer said. "You really should see the garden. It's sort of magical. And you might know something about some of the plants growing there. All April and I know is that they look pretty."

Rosalie stood and followed me through the kitchen and into the back yard. The garden lay at the far end of the yard, walled off with weathered stone and thick ivy and a stunning gate custom made by a local craftsman.

As we followed the stepstones to the gate, the wind stirred the chimes hanging from the arbor, sending a cascade of soft notes drifting through the air. The gate creaked as I pushed it open, and I led her inside.

She stopped and took in everything. In a hushed voice, she said, "Enchanting."

Doyle materialized beside the fountain, looking as much at home here as he did in the study surrounded by books.

"Have you read *The Secret Garden*?" I asked Rosalie, leading her down the path to the herb garden.

"As a child. I don't remember much about it." She stopped next to a rose bush covered in pink blooms and leaned in for a smell. "But this feels like it's right from the book. You've done an amazing job."

"Thank you."

Doyle nodded approvingly. "Charming. I do believe that Frances Hodgson Burnett herself would approve."

That was high praise, especially coming from him.

Rosalie wandered along the path, brushing her fingers along the leaves of lavender and lemon balm. "This is lovely," she murmured. "I would spend all my time out here if I were you."

"It's good for the soul." I pointed to a patch of trailing greenery. "Any idea what that is? The gardener who helped design the space left me a list of all the plants, but I have no idea which is which, except for the roses and the lemon tree, of course."

She leaned in for a closer look. "I think that's Creeping Jenny."

I asked her to identify several more plants before asking, "Does gelsemium grow in California?"

If the question surprised her, she didn't let on. "It might, but it wouldn't thrive here. It's native to the southeastern U.S." As she continued down the path she commented on different plants and flowers until she stopped and turned to me. "That's the second time you've asked me about gelsemium."

"You and Sir Arthur Conan Doyle both said it has medicinal qualities. Did you use it in your tonic?"

She expelled a puff of air. "Alright. Yes. In very small doses, it can be very effective in easing certain types of pain. Migraines. Neuralgia."

Doyle perked up. "Precisely! Fascinating results, especially when combined with—"

Rosalie continued talking. "But the amounts I use are one-thousandth of what it would take to kill someone."

"Even someone with a heart condition? Or on prescription medication?"

"It's still safe in the doses I used." She hesitated. "*Probably.* But that's why I told Irene not to share it with anyone. Especially Delilah."

Doyle gave me a smug look. "I was right all along. Irene is the murderess!"

"You specifically told her not to share it with

Delilah?" I asked. "Try to remember. It might be important."

She frowned. "I don't have to try to remember. That's exactly what I told her."

"Well, she ignored your warning, or maybe she forgot, because she admitted she let Delilah have some of it." A lightness came over me. Delilah's death was nothing more than an unfortunate accident caused by an interaction between the gelsemium in the tonic and Delilah's prescription medication.

"That's terrible," Rosalie's hand flew to her chest. "If my tonic killed Delilah, then it's my fault she's dead."

"Not at all. If it's anyone's fault, it's Irene's." Relief washed over me. I didn't have a house full of murder suspects, just people who had made questionable decisions. It could have happened to anyone, well, anyone who didn't follow instructions when given a warning. "At least now we know why Delilah felt tired and was slurring her words before she died."

Rosalie's eyes narrowed. "She was slurring her words?"

"Yes, when she asked me if there was somewhere she could rest. It almost seemed like it was a struggle for her to talk."

"I'm not a doctor, but that doesn't sound like a drug interaction."

Uh oh.

I reached into my pocket and pulled out the bottle Irene had given me. "You're saying that the amount of gelsemium you put into this bottle wouldn't cause someone to slur their speech even if they had some kind of interaction."

Rosalie spoke firmly and without reservation. "No."

I held the bottle out to her. "Why don't you have some?"

She recoiled like I'd offered her a scorpion in a teacup.

"What's wrong? I thought you said it was safe."

"It was safe when I gave it to Irene," she snapped. "But someone could've tampered with it."

Doyle stepped forward, arms crossed and gave her the most judgmental glare I'd seen from a ghost. "A convenient excuse."

"Maybe," I murmured, but Rosalie wasn't panicked or defensive. She was angry. Did that mean she was innocent?

"Yeah, I don't blame you for not drinking it." I turned the pretty little bottle over in my hand. "And by the way, if you had agreed to taste it, I would have stopped you. I don't need another dead body to deal with."

Her shoulders dropped slightly, the fight leaving her like air escaping from a balloon.

"Yes, of course," Doyle said with the attitude of someone who's just had a revelation. "Someone added an additional dose of gelsemium to the tonic."

I gave him the stink eye, but he didn't notice. "It's entirely possible that Irene was the intended victim and you were set up to take the blame."

Her mouth dropped open. "For murder?"

The question hung in the air. "Why don't we go

back inside. And let's not say anything about this to the others for now."

Her expression was grim. "If you're right, that means Greg or Todd tried to kill Irene. And if that's true, how do we know they won't try again?"

I didn't like saying it out loud, but what choice did I have? "We don't."

As I closed the door to the garden, Doyle floated beside me, his voice low and grave. "Everything points to Rosalie. She has motive. Means. Knowledge."

"You go ahead," I told Rosalie. "I need to get something from the garage."

She walked slowly to the back door, glancing over her shoulder at me before going inside and leaving me alone with Doyle.

I didn't know what to think. "She had the perfect opportunity to blame Delilah's death on an accidental interaction, but she didn't."

"Perhaps she didn't consider the implications of what she told you," Doyle said.

Rosalie didn't seem like the sort of person who spoke without thinking. After pacing back and forth across the lawn, I gave up trying to figure out what the new information meant. I stepped into the kitchen as Irma walked in with her deck of cards and a mischievous glint in her eye.

"When the guys get back," she said, "I figured I'd give them a chance to win back what they lost. You in?"

"Maybe later. Right now, I need to think."

"Think about what?"

"Oh, I don't know. The body upstairs? The fact that

I have murder suspects under my roof? That reminds me. Keep your eyes on our guests, especially Greg and Todd, and let me know if you think they might have put something in someone's food or drink, especially Irene's. Tell Jennifer to keep her eyes open, too."

Her brows pulled together. "You're serious."

"Dead serious."

CHAPTER 19

I poured myself another cup of tea while Irma rearranged the spice shelf. She must have been really bored.

I got settled on my stool and began thinking out loud. "If I could only figure out how to get the truth out of the four of them."

"Pull each into a room one at a time and interrogate them?" Irma asked without turning around. "You know, with a hundred-watt bulb shining in their face."

Doyle hovered over me. "If I had the ability to question them directly, I would get to the truth in minutes."

"That's it!" I spun to face the ghost, nearly elbowing my teacup off the counter.

Irma looked up. "That's what?"

"Oh… sometimes I forget you can't hear the ghosts. Must be nice." I waved vaguely in the air like that would help. "Doyle just gave me an idea."

The ghost leaned against the counter looking full of himself, for a moment reminding me of Chef Emile.

"Yes?" Irma's gruff voice brought me back to the present.

"Let's hold another séance. But this time, we'll be in charge."

Irma's eyes lit up. "Now you're talking! Should I get my turban?"

"Absolutely not." I wasn't sure she heard me because she was out the back door before I'd finished my two-word sentence. Moments later, I heard the unmistakable sound of her old Cadillac roaring to life.

In record time, she returned wearing a flowing purple robe that may or may not have once been a curtain and a pair of earrings that looked like they could pick up satellite radio.

And a turban. One that sparkled like she'd gotten carried away with a Bedazzler.

"The eighties called," I deadpanned. "They want their rhinestones back."

She twirled dramatically. "You know what I always say. Go big or go home."

Greg's voice from the front room told us that he and Todd had returned.

"Get Jennifer and fill her in on the plan," I whispered. "I'll meet you in the study in five minutes."

The men had news about the closure. "Looks like the county finally sent a crew," Todd said. "They're clearing the road now. It should be open in a couple of hours."

"Great news." I was more than ready to have my tearoom back. Although getting rid of my newest ghostly guest might take a little longer.

Irene and Rosalie were equally excited and started chattering about what they were going to do when they got home.

I clapped my hands. "If I may have everyone's attention. I have something planned for this afternoon while we wait for the road to reopen. Irma and I are going to hold another séance and try one more time to connect to Delilah's spirit. You are all welcome to join us."

Greg raised an eyebrow. "Last night you were dead set against a séance. In fact, you said you *forbade* it. Why the change in attitude?"

"I should have told you my reasoning sooner." I adopted a solemn expression. "You see, I have a unique sensitivity to the spirit world. Normally I avoid any formal attempts at communication. There are..." I paused dramatically, "risks."

Todd looked concerned. Greg looked intrigued. Irma looked delighted.

"Irma and I had a long talk, and she convinced me I'm strong enough to resist crossing over. She'll anchor me. Spiritually."

Irma nodded like this was all completely normal. "I've tethered many a lost soul in my time."

I refrained from asking her when, exactly, she'd done that. Before she met me her experience with spirits was limited to reruns of *Ghost Whisperer.*

"I have a gift." I was laying it on thickly, but I couldn't help myself. "And I've realized it's wrong not to use it in service of my fellow man. And woman."

Greg stood. "I'm game."

The others had varying opinions, Todd apparently

the skeptic of the group. He finally decided it might ease the boredom and agreed to join in.

We gathered in the study, where I led them past the white-shrouded table where Delilah had eaten her last meal. Irma drew the curtains while Jennifer lit a dozen candles. The flickering candlelight cast eerie shadows on the walls.

Once we were all seated, Irma took the lead, instructing us to hold hands. She raised her gaze to the ceiling and spoke in her most melodramatic voice. "Spirits of the beyond, we summon thee!"

Doyle, pacing behind her like a coach preparing for a championship game, muttered, "Oh, for heaven's sake."

Irma continued. "Let the veil between worlds part!"

Todd mumbled something about how ridiculous the whole thing was. Irene shushed him.

"We summon the spirit of Delilah, Delilah…" she leaned over to Greg who sat on her left. "What was her last name?"

"Smith," he whispered.

"We summon the spirit of Delilah Smith, whose life was so tragically cut short. If you have not moved *on*, then speak to us. Speak to us, Delilah. We seek the truth that only you can tell."

Silence filled the room, interrupted only by Todd shifting in his chair.

Irma turned her gaze on him and her tone became scolding. "The spirits will not visit us if they sense the vibration of a nonbeliever. We must all open our minds to the endless possibilities of this realm and the realm beyond."

She continued, returning to her otherworldly voice. "Delilah, speak to us. If you cannot appear in your own form or speak in your own voice, use the channel we have provided for you. Speak through her."

I slumped in my chair dramatically and let my head loll to one side. After a few moments, I sat bolt upright, spine stiff as a poker.

In a deep voice, I did my best to sound mysterious while faking a British accent. "Why have you summoned me?"

Greg's eyes were wide. "Delilah, is that you?"

"I am the spirit of Sir Arthur Conan Doyle."

Everyone at the table gasped, except perhaps Todd. I had a feeling he was rolling his eyes.

Irma leaned forward. "Sir Conan Doyle. You've been dead for many years. How can you possibly help us solve this mystery?"

Doyle puffed up his chest. "Because I am the greatest mystery writer of all time."

I repeated his words, adding, "with the possible exception of Agatha Christie." I could imagine Doyle scowling at me. "And…" Dramatic pause. "I have been watching you all since the moment you entered this house."

Greg swallowed hard. Todd looked like he wanted to take notes.

"Tell us, Sir Conan Doyle." Irma paused for dramatic effect. "Was Delilah murdered?"

"Yes."

"How?"

Doyle's haughty voice interrupted my flow. "She was poisoned!"

"Gelsemium." I sat up straighter, mimicking Doyle's smug expression. "A substance I know a great deal about."

"Are you saying she was *poisoned*?" Irma asked in a hushed voice.

Before I could answer, a chill swept through the room. Several candles flickered violently and then went out. An unfamiliar voice, a man's voice, filled my ears.

"Well," the voice said. "Isn't this a kick in the teeth."

My eyes flew open, and I groaned at the sight of a man with dark hair and glittering dark eyes standing in front of the bookcase. His suit, high starched collar, and cravat told me he'd lived around the same time as Doyle.

"I escaped death a hundred times," the man said cheerfully, "only to end up proving the mediums right.

"Harry?" Doyle wore a huge grin and hurried over to greet the ghostly newcomer. The two men shook hands vigorously while expressing their delight and surprise in running into each other so unexpectedly.

Irma's worried voice reminded me where I was. Expectant faces watched as I did my best to compose myself.

I cleared my throat. "Um… what was the question?"

Doyle shook Harry by the shoulder. "You mocked me for years."

"April?" Irma prompted again, leaning closer. "Is Sir

Arthur Conan Doyle going to finish answering the question? Was Delilah poisoned?"

I focused on the mortals in the room. "Delilah was…" I paused, distracted by the two ghosts and their very loud conversation.

"April?" Irma repeated. "Is everything okay?"

I held up my index finger. "Just a second." I waved at Harry. "Excuse me, Harry-whoever-you-are. What are you doing in my house? It's not enough I have Sir Arthur Greatest-Mystery-Author-of-all-Time Conan Doyle haunting me, but now he's invited a friend?"

Everyone was staring now, but I didn't care.

"This." Doyle gestured to Harry, "Is the one and only Harry Houdini."

CHAPTER 20

H*arry Houdini?*

I leaned back in my chair and blew out a breath. Could this weekend get any weirder?

"You've got to be kidding me." I looked from Doyle to Harry and back to Doyle. "Why? Why is he here?"

"What is it?" Jennifer got up from her chair and rushed to my side. "Can I get you anything?"

"Yes. An exorcist." I sighed. "Or a glass of water."

"Water I can do." Jennifer slipped out of the room.

"What is going on?" Greg demanded.

Houdini strolled over to the table. "Who does that guy think he is?"

I said the only thing I could think of. "This séance is over."

Greg clapped politely as everyone started talking at once. Irene wanted to know where the ghost went, while Todd congratulated Irma and I on a great performance.

"You almost had me fooled," he said with a grin.

Irma shooed everyone out of the room. "Show's over, folks. We need a moment here." When Irene lagged, she became even more insistent. "Out! Now!"

Irma's expression was so full of concern that I didn't wait for Jennifer to return before telling Irma what I'd seen. "We have a new ghost. Or, I suppose I should say, *I* have a new ghost."

Jennifer heard the last words as she returned with my water. "Oh, April. Just when you thought you were ghost-free. Who is he? Or she?"

"He claims to be Harry Houdini."

"Claims to be?" Harry huffed as if I'd said something offensive.

Jennifer gasped. "*The* Harry Houdini? The escape artist? I wish I could see him. What does he look like?"

I gave her a quick description ending with, "He's shorter than Doyle."

"But smarter," Houdini said, which started a debate between the two ghosts about their intelligence.

I put my hands over my ears trying to tune them out as best as I could. "I have no idea why he's here. Apparently, he and Doyle were friends when they were alive."

Doyle stopped arguing for long enough to tell me, "I wouldn't call us friends. Acquaintances really. Rivals in some way."

"Fine." I huffed, my frustration growing.

"They had a rivalry about the occult," Jennifer, the history expert, explained. "Doyle was convinced that there was an afterlife, and Houdini challenged him to prove it."

"I preferred facts," Houdini replied. "Still do."

"I'd still like to know what you're doing here in my study. Did you just decide to pop in on your old frenemy?"

Houdini lifted his chin arrogantly. "I'll answer that question if you tell me why he is here." Houdini gestured to Doyle.

"Interesting story, that," Doyle said. "Apparently, decades after I wrote my last book, there are fan clubs all around the world celebrating my genius. A group of them were in this very study last night, and they summoned me."

Houdini frowned. "You say they were fans of yours?"

"More like fans of Sherlock Holmes," I clarified.

Houdini was delighted by this information. "Your fictional 'consulting detective' who you tried to kill off? You couldn't keep him dead then, and now he's outlived you. And outshone you."

Jennifer tried to follow the conversation, not easy when she could only hear my side. "Is *he* helping us, too?"

"Helping with what?" Houdini asked. "What have you got yourself wrapped up in, old man? Some sort of literary dilemma?"

"A murder." Doyle's eyes shone bright with excitement. "A real-life mystery, one that these fine ladies require my expertise to solve."

I rolled my eyes, which made Jennifer giggle. "Between the two of them, I may lose my mind before we find the truth."

Doyle cleared his throat. "April, I insist we review the case from the beginning. For Mr. Houdini's benefit."

After repeating his demand to Irma and Jennifer, I told Doyle that I didn't see how his pal could help. "We're just wasting time."

"Maybe." Irma said. "But I don't think it would hurt to go over what we know so far. You never know. Having a couple of ghosts who can go around eavesdropping without any risk of being caught might help."

"She's right, April," Jennifer agreed.

"Fine." I knew when I was outnumbered. "I'll give you the condensed version."

I launched into the summary. When I got to, "Assuming the cause of death is gelsemium—"

Doyle interrupted me. "I can attest to that, being an expert on poisons." He turned to Houdini. "Have you read the paper I wrote on the subject?"

I cleared my throat to get their attention. "Delilah's death may have been from heart failure or some other natural cause, but if the gelsemium is to blame, here are the possible theories as I see them. Theory one: Rosalie made the tonic with a tiny amount of gelsemium and gave it to Irene. Irene gave some to Delilah to help with a headache. There was an interaction with one of Delilah's medication or possibly an allergic reaction, and there you have it. Accidental death by herb."

Houdini came closer and pulled a card from behind my ear. "The queen of diamonds."

I sighed. "Is this really the time for card tricks? If

you can just focus for a few more minutes, you can go back to practicing your illusions."

"Very well." A smile played on his lips.

"Theory two is that Rosalie put a lethal amount of gelsemium in the tonic, enough to kill the next person who drank it. If that's the case, then that must mean that Rosalie tried to kill Irene. Delilah was poisoned when Irene shared the tonic with her."

"Interesting." Houdini nodded slowly. "In both scenarios, the deceased was not the intended victim. Isn't it possible that Delilah may have been the person the murderer planned to kill all along?"

"Yes, of course," Doyle said. "We were discussing that very thing earlier. Go on with theory number three."

Number three? Had we gotten that far? "Well…if the poison was meant for Delilah, then… I would think Irene would have to know about it. And Rosalie would have been the one to put it in the tonic. Maybe they were in it together?"

"Brilliant!" Doyle said.

"But wrong." Houdini added, and Doyle quickly agreed.

"They don't like theory number three," I told Irma and Jennifer. "What about you two? Theory one, two, or three?"

Jennifer liked number one, while Irma voted for two. The ghosts wanted to throw out all my theories and start over.

"But why?" I asked, getting close to my wits end.

Doyle tutted. "Every mystery has a second twist."

"This isn't a mystery novel," I reminded him.

Irma grumbled. "If it were, it would be lot more fun. And there would be a handsome detective. And a chase scene with a few explosions."

"What kind of books are you reading?" I tried to get us back on track. "Everyone says that the simplest solution is usually the correct one. But which one is simplest?"

Houdini rubbed his hands together and grinned. "I suggest there is a simpler solution that we are yet to consider. I propose a bet. Doyle? What's the wager?"

While they worked out how much to bet, Irma turned to me. "Sometimes people do stupid things for dumb reasons and leave behind a big mess instead of neatly tied clues."

"Exactly," I said. "And if someone did something stupid, whether they meant to kill someone or not, we still need some sort of evidence or proof."

Houdini held up a silver dollar, then made it vanish with a flourish. "Perhaps someone used sleight of hand to make it appear that Rosalie did it."

"Not everything is misdirection and hidden trapdoors," Doyle grumbled.

"Ha!" Houdini crossed the room until he was nose to nose with the other ghost. "So says the man who once claimed a fairy photograph proved the existence of supernatural beings."

Doyle glared at Houdini. "Anyone could have slipped poison into a cup when no one was looking. Or a teapot." He lifted the lid of one of the china teapots and said, "Voila!" To my surprise, he pulled out a rabbit with floppy ears. "See what I mean? Even I can do magic tricks now that I'm a spirit."

Houdini gave him a thoughtful look. "I see what you're saying, though I'm not sure it disproves my point. Either way, the question is: How do we solve this mystery?"

Doyle raised his chin in the air. "One must simply have the talent for crime solving, something you clearly do not possess."

"Very well. I accept your challenge. I will return with the name of the perpetrator and the proof needed to put them behind bars." Houdini turned to me and bowed deeply. "It was a pleasure to make your acquaintance. I'm off to see what I can see. And hear what I can hear."

Houdini disappeared through the wall and Doyle followed.

"The game is afoot," I said with relief. "They're gone. For now, at least."

CHAPTER 21

Sitting in a ghost-free room was a welcome change, but I could hardly stay in the study and enjoy the peace and quiet knowing one of the four people in the next room might be a murderer. "You know what I would like to do?"

"Solve the murder?" Jennifer suggested.

"Yes, eventually." I stood and rolled my shoulders trying to release some of the built-up tension. "I'd like to get some fresh air. Anyone up for a walk to the lighthouse?" I had a severe case of cabin fever from being cooped up with my unexpected guests.

"Yeah, let's blow this popsicle stand." Irma led the way through the other room, waving at the group as she passed them. "Catch ya later."

Greg and Irene looked cozy on the sofa, while Todd pretended not to watch Rosalie read her book. I let them know we'd be back in an hour or so and to help themselves to whatever was in the kitchen, adding, "As long as you clean up after yourselves."

We crossed the street and turned north along the beach path that led to the historic lighthouse. My mood improved almost immediately with the warm sun on my shoulders and cool ocean breezes, not to mention that neither of my new ghost friends had followed us.

The conversation centered on the beautiful weather and how lucky we were to live in Serenity Cove, but finally it came back around to murder.

"Doyle and Houdini don't seem to think Rosalie is responsible for Delilah's death, but it's the simplest and most obvious explanation. I lean toward it being an unfortunate accident, but then why is Rosalie so evasive?"

I stopped along the path and looked across the street, where Sarah's Bed and Breakfast stood somehow both majestic and quirky with its colorful paint job.

"Should we stop in?" Irma was already crossing the street, probably hoping Sarah had more baked goods to share.

Jennifer and I followed, climbing the front steps and stepping inside. After being out in the bright sun, it took several moments for my eyes to adjust to the dim interior. The lobby, normally bright and cheerful decorated in shades of pink, Sarah's favorite color, felt gloomy with only flameless candles to light the room.

Sarah's face lit up and she hurried over to greet us. "It's almost like I knew you were coming. I have a pot of coffee brewing and a fresh batch of muffins."

"But I thought you had an electric stove. Is the power back on?" I asked.

She shook her head. "We bought a gas-powered generator after that huge storm. We can hardly run our B&B without power, and the last thing I want is everyone leaving."

I chuckled. "That's the one thing I *do* want. I've been stuck with some of the members of the group that hired us for the Sherlock Holmes event. And they can't leave until the road opens."

"Oh, dear. I'm used to having guests, but that must be a challenge for you. Why don't you stay and relax for a bit?" She led us to a secluded table in the small dining area, perhaps sensing we'd like privacy. Moments later, she returned with a basket of muffins, plates, three mugs, napkins, and a carafe tucked under her arm.

"I would have needed three trips to carry all that," I said as she filled our mugs with steaming hot coffee.

"How was the event?" Sarah asked, making small talk.

"It was great until the earthquake," I said. "Luckily everyone had left except the board members. Their treasurer stayed with you last night. Rosalie."

"Ah yes. Lovely young lady." She gave a little chuckle. "These days I call anyone younger than me a young lady."

"It was lucky you had a room for her on such short notice."

"Yes, it was. Although I wouldn't really call four weeks short notice. Even so, she got the last room." She stood. “I’ve got a couple of loafs of carrot bread in the oven, so I’d better keep an eye on it. Make yourself comfortable for as long as you like and let me know if I can get you anything else.”

“Stopping in here was the best idea you’ve had in a while, April,” Irma said as she stuffed a huge chunk of a carrot walnut muffin into her mouth.

I lowered my voice in case anyone was close enough to overhear us. “Rosalie lied. She said when she left the event yesterday, she stopped here on an impulse and Sarah just happened to have a room.”

“Maybe there’s a reason why she lied,” Jennifer said. “I mean a reason other than trying to cover up that she’d given a bottle of poisoned tonic to Irene. An innocent reason.”

“Like what?” I asked.

She sipped her coffee as she thought this over. “You know how Todd watches her all the time like a lovesick puppy? Maybe she thought if he knew she’d planned to stay overnight, he’d pressure her into letting him stay with her. And maybe she’s not ready for that.”

Irma nodded. “Or maybe she’s not at all interested in him. Oh! And maybe he found out she was staying here and decided to frame her for murder.”

“Interesting.” I found her logic hard to follow, but I still wanted to hear her out. “You’re suggesting he killed Delilah just to frame Rosalie for murder?”

“Of course not. I’m suggesting he figured he could get rid of Delilah and also frame Rosalie. Two birds, one stone.”

"Okay, I get his motive for framing Rosalie, but why did he kill Delilah?"

Irma frowned. "Do I have to figure everything out for you? You're the head sleuth. I'm just your quirky sidekick."

Jennifer gave her a quizzical look. "What does that make me?"

I jumped in before Irma could answer. "Indispensable."

Jennifer beamed while I thought about the others. "The problem is, Delilah was such an unlikable person, it's easy to imagine any of them wanting them dead. As for actual motives, Greg might have been embezzling from the group. Maybe Delilah was going to turn him in to the authorities? And then there's the love triangle. If Irene considered Delilah a rival for Greg's affection, maybe she wanted her out of the way."

"Weak motives," Irma said.

"A lot of help you are for a quirky sidekick. But you're right. It's hard to believe that young, pretty Irene was worried about competition from Delilah." I sighed. "The road is going to be open soon giving the murderer more of a chance to cover their tracks."

"I still think Rosalie did it," Irma muttered.

Without proof, it didn't matter what we thought.

CHAPTER 22

The scent of sea air followed us back from Sarah's B&B. As we approached the tearoom, Irma huffed beside me like she'd just conquered Everest instead of the gentle slope of a coastal bluff.

"I need a drink," she announced.

"I need tea," I declared. "Possibly a scone."

"I'll handle the tea," Jennifer offered. "You're on your own with the scone."

Irma scoffed. "All this time and you haven't learned how to make scones yet? What have you been doing with your spare time?"

"Working, going to school, spending time with my friends. And I know how to make scones, but for some reason April's always come out better."

Todd sat alone on the porch, slouched in one of the white wicker chairs like he'd sunk into it hours ago and wasn't quite sure how to get out.

"You two head in," I told Jennifer and Irma, giving them a little wave. "I'll be along shortly."

Irma raised one skeptical eyebrow but didn't argue. Jennifer gave me a hopeful thumbs-up behind her back.

I eased into the seat beside Todd, the wicker creaking beneath me.

"Nice breeze," I said casually.

He nodded, staring out at the sea lost in thought. We sat in silence for a minute, and I came to the conclusion if we were going to have a conversation, I'd have to start it.

"Everything okay?" I asked. "I mean besides Delilah being dead and you being still stuck here."

He shrugged, and for a moment I thought I might not get a single word out of him. I let him sit in silence until he was ready.

Finally, he said, "I'm worried. About Rosalie mostly."

"You're worried she might be accused of murder?"

"She's already been accused." He shot me a glare. "Thanks to you."

"Oh." I had to admit he was right in a way. "I just want to find out what really happened to Delilah. If you can help me find out the truth, then I can clear Rosalie of suspicion before the police and the coroner finally arrive." I paused. "I know how much you care about her."

His shoulders dropped and the anger left his expression. "I don't think she cares about me other than as a friend."

"Friendship can turn into something more. Maybe

if you gave her some space. Like…" I hesitated. "Don't hover so much?"

His eyes widened. "Have I been hovering?" He sighed. "I didn't mean too, I've just been worried about her, and she won't tell me how she's feeling."

"She doesn't have to tell anyone what she's feeling." I softened my tone, realizing that might sound harsh to him. "And anyway, she might not know how she feels. Can I ask you something?" He didn't say no, so I forged on. "You don't seem nearly as passionate about Sherlock Holmes as the others, so how did you get involved with the group?" It felt like a long time before he answered.

"She gave me a job," he said finally. "Delilah. When no one else would."

"Why couldn't you get a job?"

He turned to me, eyes squinting against the early afternoon sun. "I had a drug problem. In and out of rehab for years. In and out of jail, too. Petty crimes, that sort of thing. I'd been clean for almost a year, but I was struggling, hanging by a thread. When no one will give you a chance…"

"I'm glad she helped you," I said gently.

"Yeah, well…" He leaned forward, resting his forearms on his thighs. "After a while, I learned that was her thing. She liked to rescue people. But not out of the kindness of her heart. Maybe that's how it started, but she liked surrounding herself with people she could look down on. Who she could control."

I didn't know what to say, so I stayed quiet, hoping he'd say more.

"She called it redemption." His lip curled at the word. "But it came with strings. Invisible ones, until you tried to move in a direction she didn't like."

"She held things over your head?"

He nodded. "Just enough to make sure you remembered who pulled you out of the gutter. And her cruel comments were balanced with praise, so you were always off kilter."

Jennifer stepped onto the porch carrying two mugs of hot tea. She set them down and scurried off.

I held the mug to my lips, taking a sip as I inhaled the steam. "Do you think she had something on the others?"

Todd looked away. "I know a little about Rosalie's secret. It's not mine to tell."

"Of course not."

"And there's no way Greg would have put up with the way she talked to him otherwise. For the past year, she's been saying she was going to step down as President and let him take over. And then, yesterday I overheard her tell him she'd changed her mind. He was too irresponsible with money. She wasn't wrong about that." He chuckled.

"What's so funny?"

"I wonder if Irene would be as interested in Greg if she knew he was pretty much broke. I think he was forced to resign from his law firm. I don't know the details, but I'm sure Delilah did."

"I see." The sun ducked behind a cloud and the temperature quickly dropped a few degrees. I rubbed my arms, wishing I had a sweater but not wanting to leave until I learned all I could from Todd.

He seemed mesmerized by the crashing waves, and I almost didn't want to break the spell he was in.

But I had to know. "What about Irene?"

His eyes met mine. "What about her?"

"Did Delilah rescue her?"

He seemed perplexed by the question. "She must have. Why would Irene be any different than the rest of us?"

"Delilah might have wanted to mentor her. Share her wisdom. That sort of thing."

Todd scoffed. "You didn't know Delilah."

That much was true, but I was learning more and more about her. The way she treated her board members gave all of them a motive.

He stood abruptly. "I think I'll take a walk. Clear my head."

I let him go, watching as he stepped off the porch and headed down the path toward the bluff.

CHAPTER 23

Back in the kitchen, Irma and Jennifer were chatting about Harry Houdini. Or rather, Jennifer was talking about him while Irma half listened. Meanwhile, Harry's ghost leaned against the refrigerator taking in every word.

"He was a master of illusion," Jenifer said. "And ironically, with all the magic he performed…"

"Tricks," Houdini corrected, but she couldn't hear him, of course.

"…he didn't believe in magic. Or the afterlife."

I chuckled. "That's ironic, considering he's here enjoying his afterlife in my house."

"Oh!" Jennifer looked around the room. "Is he here right now?"

I pointed to the refrigerator. "He seems to be enjoying hearing you talk about him."

"You were a very interesting man," Jennifer said. She turned back to me and continued. "He shared a lot of his secrets, like the all the ways he would hide keys.

One time, as a stunt, he got locked up in jail, and when his wife kissed him goodbye, she transferred the key from her mouth to his."

Irma grimaced. "That's doesn't sound very sanitary."

Doyle shimmered into view. "All hyperbole and showmanship if you ask me."

The teapot was still warm, so I refilled my mug and recapped my conversation with Todd for Irma and Jennifer while I mixed up a batch of scones.

"He said Delilah liked to 'rescue' people." I pulled my favorite ceramic mixing bowl from the cupboard and slid the flour canister closer. "He had what you might call a checkered past. She gave him a job, but she never let him forget he owed her."

Irma snorted. "She didn't hand out favors. She handed out IOUs."

"She might have had something on each one of them," I added, measuring out the flour and adding baking powder and salt. "Todd is convinced he wasn't the only one. Although he's not as sure about Irene."

Irma yawned. "I'm going upstairs for a nap. If anything happens, like another murder, wake me."

Jennifer gasped. "Don't even say that! I thought you knew better than to tempt fate."

Irma padded off, mumbling something about how fate didn't need tempting. Jennifer stayed put as I grabbed the cream from the fridge and added it to the flour mixture.

"There's something about baking that helps me think. Plus, we still have clotted cream in the fridge. Might as well use it before it goes bad."

I gathered the dough into a sticky ball, then set it on a silicon mat. I was patting it into an even thickness when Rosalie appeared in the doorway.

She hesitated. "Are you baking?"

"Scones." I gave her a small smile. "I thought it might be a good time for something warm and comforting."

Rosalie's eyes brightened. "I meant to tell you the scones you served yesterday were delicious. Do you mind if I watch?"

"Not at all," I said. "Jennifer was just about to go upstairs, so it would be nice to have company."

Jennifer got the hint. "Yes, I was about to go up to my room for a nap."

She scurried away before I could thank her.

"This is my favorite recipe. Just five ingredients—flour, baking soda, a teaspoon or two of sugar, a pinch of salt and heavy cream. I asked Delilah if she wanted me to make 'No Sugar Sherlock Scones, but she didn't care for the idea."

"But that's so clever!"

"Thank you." I was happy to have someone appreciate one of my puns. "I didn't bother testing to see if the scones would still taste good without the sugar, but I thought I might as well do that now. It might be a nice addition to the menu, and I could serve them with sugar free jam. Clotted cream is already sugar free."

Rosalie watched me as I cut out a dozen scones, setting them on the baking sheet. I combined the scraps and repeated the process cutting out three more.

I brushed the tops with milk, and soon they were in the oven with the timer set.

"My favorite thing about scones is how quick and easy they are to make and how few ingredients they take. I can go from thinking 'scones would be nice' and then, twenty minutes later, I'm eating them."

"I'd love your recipe," Rosalie said. "Unless it's a trade secret."

"Not at all. I'm thinking of putting together a cookbook. *SereniTea Tearoom Treats*, or something like that."

She grinned. "You totally should."

"Would you like another cup of tea? That's not the only thing we ever drink in this house, but we do drink a lot of it. And by 'we' I mean 'me'."

She asked if I had more of the herbal tea I'd served at the event. Since it came in teabags, I made her a single cup and set it on the island in front of her.

"I spoke to Todd briefly a little while ago." I carefully broached the subject I wanted to ask about. "I don't need to know the details. But… did Delilah use something against you?"

Rosalie stopped with her mug halfway to her mouth, then set it back down.

"Yes." She stared at the steam curling from the cup. "A mistake I made a long time ago."

I waited, not pushing, hoping she'd say more.

"I've spent years trying to move on from it," she continued. "I thought it was behind me. But Delilah… she had a way of bringing things up when you'd almost forgotten about it. And she made sure you knew she had the upper hand."

"I see."

Her eyes finally lifted to mine. "But it wasn't a secret worth killing over. If that's what you were getting at."

"Sorry." I truly was sorry. "I didn't mean to sound like I was accusing you of anything. I'm just trying to get to the truth."

Rosalie exhaled, her shoulders relaxing slightly. "The truth is that Delilah had a heart attack or maybe a stroke. Or an aneurism. And it couldn't have happened to a better person." She shrugged. "You must be shocked to hear me say that."

"Not at all. No one seems to be mourning her as far as I can see." A thought occurred to me. "Has anyone contacted her family?"

"She didn't have any children. If she has any relatives still living, they'd be distant cousins or nieces or nephews."

Sir Arthur Conan Doyle had returned but without Houdini. He leaned against the doorway, arms crossed, brow furrowed in ghostly contemplation.

"She seems sincere," he murmured. "I'm inclined to believe her, but she may simply be an excellent actress, much like Stapleton in *The Hound of the Baskervilles*."

I tried to keep from smiling as I remembered my conversation with Irene.

Rosalie gave me a curious look. "What's so funny?"

"Something I remembered. I get the impression that Irene is not as much of a fan of Sherlock Holmes as she says."

"Oh, you mean like, 'I like books with dogs?'"

I had to bite my lip to keep from laughing. “If she mentions a basset hound, that’s my fault.”

She broke into a huge grin. “Like *The Basset Hound of the Baskervilles*?”

I pressed my hand over my mouth and nodded.

We were still giggling when Irene pushed the kitchen door open. “What are you guys laughing about?”

I had to think fast. “I was telling Rosalie about the time I filled a sugar bowl with salt instead of sugar. You should have seen everyone’s faces, but I couldn’t figure out what was wrong.”

“Oh.” Irene forced a smile, but that only made Rosalie laugh more.

Doyle raised one eyebrow. “I do not understand why you are making jokes instead of getting to the bottom of this investigation.” He huffed and walked through the door, probably in search of Houdini.

My own laughter faded as I remembered that one of these two charming young women might be a murderer.

CHAPTER 24

After the scones had time to cool, Rosalie followed me into the front room. I set my tray of scones, clotted cream, and strawberry jam on the sideboard. There would have been lemon curd too, if my uninvited guests hadn't finished it off.

Greg lounged on the sofa reading with Irene leaning her head on his shoulder. Todd sat at a café table by the window doing his best to ignore us, especially Rosalie who went over and sat next to him.

"Here you go." I forced myself to sound cheerful. "Help yourselves. Freshly baked scones and all the fixings."

I caught a flicker of appreciation in Irene's eyes while Greg merely offered a tight smile. I turned to head back to the kitchen, but Greg stood suddenly and strode to my side.

"April, I wanted to thank you for your hospitality. You've been very generous considering the situation."

Without waiting for a response, he lowered his voice and added, "I wonder if we can have a word."

"Um, sure." I assumed he meant alone, but there was only one place I could think of where we'd have privacy. "Why don't I help you take the pictures down that Delilah had you hang in the study."

"Yes, I'd nearly forgotten about them with everything going on."

When we stepped inside the study, he looked around the room. "I can't believe it was only yesterday…" He didn't finish the sentence.

"It must be hard to imagine that you'll never see Delilah again."

He took the painting of Queen Victoria down from over the fireplace and leaned it against the wall. He hesitated, then turned to me. "You shouldn't trust Todd."

I blinked. "Excuse me?"

Greg's voice dropped further. "He's not who he seems. His past is... unsavory. If someone had reason to make sure Delilah stayed quiet, it might've been him."

I studied his expression, calm and composed, but with a flicker of tension tightening the corners of his mouth. Was it concern? Or strategy?

"A lot of people have pasts they're not proud of." I held his gaze, hoping he got my meaning. "Don't people deserve a second chance?"

Greg stiffened, his eyes narrowing. "Yes, of course. I didn't mean to say he didn't. I just thought after you've opened your home to us, you deserved to know. If something happened to you, I'd feel terrible."

"Thank you." I couldn't help but think that if I were in any danger, the warning should have been delivered yesterday rather than now as they were about to leave Serenity Cove.

He gave a short nod, then took the other paintings down, stacking them by the study door. "I'll get Todd to help me carry them to the car before we leave." I watched him return to the others with a dozen new questions dancing through my head.

The way Greg had delivered that warning felt like he was trying to throw me off the track. And the more someone tried to steer suspicion, the more I wanted to know what they were hiding.

I stepped through the kitchen door, the warm scent of scones still lingering in the air and made a mental note: keep the kettle hot... and my eyes open.

CHAPTER 25

By the time I returned to the front room to collect my tray and the dishes, the mood had curdled like cream left out too long. Greg was pacing by the front door, while the others slumped in their chairs with the air of people trapped at the world's worst party.

"Can I get anyone anything else?" I asked, but no one made a move to reply.

Greg stopped mid-step, turning toward the window as if something might appear out there to save him. Irene picked at her napkin. Rosalie was unusually still, with her hands folded tightly in her lap. Todd gave me a faint smile and a shrug.

As I collected plates, I kept my voice casual. "Just curious. Once the road reopens, are any of you planning to stay behind?"

The question hung in the air like the last note of a broken music box.

"Why would we stay?" Todd sounded belligerent as if I'd just assigned him detention.

I shrugged. "The coroner will be here as soon as the road is clear. Don't you want to know how Delilah died?"

Greg stopped pacing. Irene's head snapped up, eyes wide.

"We know how she died," Todd said firmly. "It was her heart."

"Yes, her heart," Greg echoed quickly. He smoothed the front of his vest, but the wrinkles persisted. No wonder, since he'd been wearing it since the previous day.

Rosalie scowled and turned to Irene. "What about you? Do you think she was murdered?"

Irene, clearly caught off guard, stammered, "I... I don't know."

"You don't know? So, you think she was poisoned?" Rosalie stood and looked around the room. "You're all dancing around it, but you think I did it. You think I poisoned her."

Her voice cracked like a whip through the room. Irene looked stricken. Todd opened his mouth, but nothing came out.

"I'm not sorry Delilah's dead," Rosalie went on, her voice trembling. "But I wouldn't have killed her just to —" She stopped herself, jaw clenched tight. "And you're all glad she's gone too, even if you won't say it."

Her gaze darted from face to face. No one met her eyes, and no one spoke.

"Fine. Think what you want."

She stormed out the front door, slamming it behind her.

CHAPTER 26

Todd jumped to his feet to follow her, but when he glanced back at me, I shook my head.

"I think Rosalie's nerves are fried," I said to the group. "And it's no surprise. I think all of us are a bit on edge. She just needs a little alone time and I'm sure she'll come back and apologize."

Greg sat stiffly on the edge of the settee, one knee bouncing. Irene had moved to the wingback chair by the window, hands curled tightly in her lap. Todd stared moodily at the floor.

"I have some hibiscus cooler in case you were up to your eyeballs in tea. Personally, I can drink about three pots of tea a day, but I know not everyone is like me."

"No thanks," Greg murmured, barely glancing up.

The room was littered with cups, mugs, and discarded napkins, like a teenager's room who knew that eventually Mom would come and pick up after them. I guessed that made me Mom. I carried what I could to the kitchen and returned for the rest, wondering if they'd stopped talking to each other completely.

Todd finally spoke. "She's right."

"Who's right?" Irene asked.

"Rosalie's right. This is tearing us apart."

No one responded for a moment. Then Irene gave a slow nod. "Delilah was difficult," she said carefully. "But she didn't do anything so awful to any of us that we would've done... something so terrible."

Her voice trailed off, but the word hung in the air like smoke.

Greg shifted in his chair. "She had a heart problem, and I don't need to stay to hear the coroner tell me so." He shot me a glare. "If some people hadn't suggested she might have been poisoned, it would have never entered our minds that one of us could have hurt her."

I kept my expression neutral, but it wasn't easy. "I didn't mean to accuse anyone. But you have to admit, the circumstances were odd. I just wanted to get to the bottom of what happened to Delilah. I would think you'd want that too."

Irene sat up straight in her chair. "What happened to Delilah... it's awful. But we can put it behind us and be like a family again."

Todd scoffed. "We were never anything resembling a family."

Irene seemed to become aware of my presence as if I hadn't been there the whole time. "I'd love a hibiscus cooler."

"Get it yourself," was what I wanted to say, but I

held my tongue. As I was getting her drink from the kitchen, Doyle appeared next to me, nearly making me drop the glass. "They're quite like the family in the Christie novel, *Appointment with Death*. An awful family who despised their matriarch. Sound familiar?"

When I returned and handed Irene her drink, Greg stood. "When Rosalie comes back, we need to tell her we know she had nothing to do with Delilah's death."

Todd glared at him. "I never thought she did."

I gave them a tentative smile. "If you need anything else, I'll be in the kitchen."

As I stepped out of the room, I didn't believe for a second that the tension was truly gone. But for now, the storm had passed leaving only the question that still echoed in my mind:

Was one of them going to get away with murder?

CHAPTER 27

The house felt restless. Not just the people in it, but the walls, the floors, even the air. A kind of tight, coiled tension that had nothing to do with the weather or the tea selection.

I was halfway through hand washing the dishes when the kitchen door creaked open. Greg leaned in, one hand braced against the frame.

"Any word on the road?"

"Not yet," I said. "But I'm sure we'll know something soon."

Greg exhaled heavily. "Rosalie still hasn't come back."

I wiped my hands on a dishtowel. "Maybe she just needed to cool off."

"Even so," he said. "Todd and I are going to drive around and look for her. Just to make sure she's okay." He disappeared into the other room before I could say anything else.

I powered up my phone and fired off a quick text to

Freddie:

Any update on the road? The suspects are getting itchy to leave town.

I set the phone down and it buzzed again. This time it was a text from Andy.

Why didn't you tell me someone died at your house?

I typed my answer: *You didn't give me a chance.*

As I hit send, I heard footsteps practically galloping down the main staircase. Jennifer made a surprising amount of noise for someone so petite.

Her voice came from the other room. "Are you here by yourself?"

I didn't hear Irene's reply, but I did hear Jennifer inviting her to her room. "I have the most ridiculous collection of costumes. Want to see them?"

Irene mumbled a reply, but her lack of enthusiasm didn't dampen Jennifer's spirit.

"Come on, it'll take your mind off things."

Irene must have agreed, since moments later, two pairs of footsteps trudged up the stairs.

I'd nearly finished cleaning the kitchen when Jennifer reappeared with a satisfied sparkle in her eyes.

She joined me by the sink. "I showed Irene my costume collection. She really liked the hats, so I let her try them all on. I think it cheered her up a bit."

"It's been hard on all of us, but especially them. And Irene seems drained."

Jennifer nodded. "I told her not to worry. That you've solved murders before. If someone poisoned Delilah, you'll figure it out."

I raised an eyebrow. "I hope it didn't spook her.

People don't seem to think there are murders in small towns like ours."

Jennifer shrugged, grabbing a glass of lemonade from the counter. "She laughed. Sort of. Maybe she thought I was kidding."

"Kidding?"

Who would kid about murder?

CHAPTER 28

The front door creaked open, and the sound of footsteps and excited voices filled the hallway. I went to see if the two men had returned with news.

"We talked to one of the road crew guys," Greg called out, the eagerness in his voice unmistakable. "He said the road should be clear in about an hour!"

Todd was right behind him, grinning like someone who'd just been handed a get-out-of-jail-free card. "We're finally getting out of here."

They gathered their few belongings, setting them by the door.

Greg gave Todd a friendly pat on the back. "Help me with the paintings?" When Todd didn't seem to know what he was talking about, Greg clarified, "Delilah's paintings that she brought for the event. There are a few other things in the study, too."

I returned to the kitchen and leaned against the

counter, exhaling slowly. "I'm not celebrating until we see taillights heading out of town."

"Optimism isn't a crime," Jennifer said with a wink, as she set an assortment of leftover cookies on a plate.

I grabbed one and stuffed it in my mouth in one bite and put the kettle on for what I was praying would be the final round of tea. With my guests packing up, I dared to think we might actually return to normal, whatever that looked like anymore.

Once the tea had steeped and the tray was arranged with teapot, teacups, sugar bowl, and milk pitcher, I carried it into the front room. Jennifer followed with the cookies.

Irene sat curled in an armchair like a cat unsure whether to nap or flee. Her eyes flicked up as we entered.

"Teatime again?" she asked softly.

"Would it be a proper farewell without it?" I replied, setting the tray down.

Greg and Todd entered just as I began pouring.

"We wouldn't mind a little snack before we hit the road." Greg lowered himself onto the settee.

Todd flopped into a chair and helped himself to a shortbread cookie. "It's going to be a long drive home, and I'm not stopping unless I have to."

"How long is your drive?" I said, making conversation as I poured tea into the cups.

"About three hours as long as I don't hit traffic."

I set the men's cups in front of them and carried one to Irene.

She smiled faintly. "Do you have any lemon?"

"Fresh from the lemon tree," Jennifer said. "I'll cut you some slices."

As I picked up my own cup, ready for a nice warm sip of tea, Irene suddenly coughed and then kept coughing.

She set her teacup down and gasped, "Water."

I hurried to the kitchen, filled a glass with filtered water, and hurried back to the room where Irma had just come down the stairs. Her hair was sticking up in three directions.

I managed not to snicker. "Did you have a good nap?"

"Yes." She didn't look happy, and I wondered why. Then I remembered this was Irma, whose face wore a permanent scowl.

I handed Irene the water and returned to my seat. As I lifted my teacup to finally take a sip, Irma hurried over to my side and bumped right into me, jostling my arm.

Tea sloshed over the rim of the cup, splashing down the front of my blouse and onto the rug.

"Irma!" I scolded.

"Oops," Irma said quickly, snatching the teacup from my hands before I could so much as dab at my shirt. "I'll clean that up."

She passed Jennifer with the plate of lemon slices on the way to the kitchen. Jennifer gave me a questioning look as I followed Irma, who was opening cabinets and seemed to be looking for something.

"Irma, what are you doing?"

"Shhh. I'm looking for somewhere to hide your teacup and what's left of the tea."

I stared at the half empty cup on the counter, my heart giving a faint, uneasy thud.

Irma finally turned, her gaze steady and sharp. "You might want to test it. Just in case. And from now on, we do not leave our cups unattended, do you understand?"

I understood a little too well.

CHAPTER 29

Jennifer's voice drifted softly from the front room. She was chatting with Irene, probably explaining which version of *Pride and Prejudice* was the best. Irene's laugh was tentative, and I doubted she shared Jennifer's passion for Jane Austen. Greg and Todd had gone out on the porch for one last look at the ocean view.

Irma grabbed the glass cleaner and several microfiber cloths, saying the windows needed a good cleaning, but I knew she was looking out for Jennifer. She didn't trust any of them, and I didn't blame her.

I set the kettle back on to boil and let out a slow breath. For the first time in what felt like hours, I had a moment to myself.

There I went tempting fate again.

With a flicker in the corner of my vision, Sir Arthur Conan Doyle and Harry Houdini appeared side by side like mismatched bookends.

"We've done it." Doyle straightened his cravat.

I sighed, not bothering to hide my weariness. "Done what?"

"We've solved it," Houdini said, arms folded. "Case closed."

"Oh?" I crossed my arms, mirroring his posture. "Do tell."

Doyle stepped forward, all puffed-up certainty. "The four of them. Greg, Irene, Todd, and Rosalie. They worked together to bring about Delilah's demise."

I blinked. "You mean like in *The Orient Express*?"

"Oh, yes. I suppose." Doyle didn't appear thrilled by the comparison to the Agatha Christie novel, but he didn't let that stop him. "Each had a role. Each had a reason. A shared motive to silence Delilah before she could expose whatever she had on each one of them. Once she was gone, they would all be free."

"But—" I raised a hand. "Hold that thought."

I grabbed one of the last shortbread cookies and sat down, needing a moment to think. The voices outside the kitchen had faded into a background hum, like a radio turned low.

Were the two ghosts right? Is that what I'd been missing all along?

"Okay, let's look at all the clues, one by one." I took a bite and felt the buttery crumbly cookie practically melt in my mouth. "Jennifer overheard Delilah say to Irene, 'If you don't tell him, I will.'"

The rest of the puzzle pieces came together in rapid-fire succession: the wiped teacup that should've had Delilah's signature red lipstick. The bottle of tonic Rosalie swore had only trace amounts of gelsemium but later refused to drink. Irene's insistence that she hadn't shared her tonic, that she'd thrown it away. All lies.

I turned to Doyle who watched me carefully. "Does gelsemium have a taste?"

Doyle didn't miss a beat. "Bitter. Metallic. With a faint floral note. Quite distinct if you know what you're looking for."

I rose, crossed the kitchen, and opened the small cabinet near the sink. There, behind a stack of recipe cards, was the teacup Irma had tucked away.

Warily, I dipped my little finger into the cup and touched it to my tongue. At first, I didn't taste a thing, and then I detected just a hint of something.

Bitter.

Distinct.

Deadly.

I pulled out my phone and tapped Freddie's number first.

"April?" Her voice was laced with static and fatigue.

"I think I know who poisoned Delilah, but they're going to leave as soon as the road opens."

"I see." She paused then said, "Leave it to me."

"Should I call Andy, I mean Sheriff Fontana?"

"I'll handle that."

Setting the teacup back in its hiding place, I turned to Doyle and Houdini. "You could be right, and they're all in on it, but I don't think the four of them could team up to put together a jigsaw puzzle, much less a murder."

Houdini appeared disappointed.

Doyle gave me a haughty look. "You believe a criminal mastermind performed the deed on their own?"

"She's no criminal mastermind, that's for sure, but yes." I dropped my voice to a whisper. "I believe Irene poisoned Delilah without any help from the others."

And I might be her next target.

CHAPTER 30

Houdini and Doyle wanted proof, which I couldn't provide, but I had plenty of evidence pointing directly at Irene.

I stepped into the other room just as Greg and Todd came through the front door. I wanted to talk to Irma, but I'd have to insist that Jennifer join us. No way was I going to let anything happen to her if Irene started dispensing poison willy nilly.

Greg walked over to Irene. "Why don't we take a walk before our long drive. We'll be cooped up in the car for several hours."

Irene slowly stood but seemed unsteady on her feet.

"I feel a little… woozy." Her voice wavered and she reached out for the arm of the chair to steady herself.

Greg caught Irene as her knees buckled. She crumpled into his arms, her head lolling to the side like a rag doll.

"Irene?" he gasped, lowering her gently onto the sofa.

Irma shoved Greg out of the way and sank to her knees, her fingers already at Irene's wrist. "She has a pulse."

"Thank goodness," Greg said with relief.

Todd hovered uncertainly, wringing his hands. "We need to call someone."

"There will be a doctor here as soon as the road opens. I've already called her several times."

My eyes locked onto the half-empty teacup sitting on the low table near Irene's chair, her pale lipstick visible on the rim.

While the others hovered around Irene, I picked up the cup, careful not to draw attention, and carried it into the kitchen. My heart pounded in my ears, but my hands remained steady.

As the door swung closed behind me, I set the cup on the counter, took a breath, and dipped the tip of a spoon into the liquid. Then, bracing myself, I touched the spoon to my tongue.

This time I recognized the taste instantly. Bitter, metallic, and medicinal.

Poison.

CHAPTER 31

I set the spoon down with a trembling hand, then touched the side of the cup, which felt lukewarm. The poison had been added recently.

But Rosalie wasn't even in the house.

Which meant...

My thoughts turned like a carousel. Greg hovered protectively over Irene. Todd, always just on the edge of the group, listened and observed. Either of them could have slipped something into her cup. But why?

And if one of them had poisoned Irene's tea, then they must have been the one who poisoned Delilah. That was the only thing that made sense. Did Irene know one of them was guilty and might betray their deadly secret?

I leaned heavily against the counter, the cozy warmth of the room suddenly replaced by an icy dread. Had the poisoner just struck again—right in front of me?

"I thought for sure Irene had poisoned Delilah," I murmured. "Looks like I was wrong."

"Well!" came a voice behind me. "That's a refreshing admission."

I swung around in time to see Sir Arthur Conan Doyle shimmer into view looking smug enough to burst the buttons on his ghostly waistcoat. Houdini walked through the wall, tossing a ghostly coin from hand to hand.

"I do love being right," Doyle said with a sniff.

"She could still be the killer," Houdini offered. "Perhaps it's all an act. Stage fainting was very popular in my day."

I shook my head. "I'm almost positive that was gelsemium in her teacup. So, unless she wanted to do herself in..." I struggled to put the pieces together. It was like someone had mixed pieces from two jigsaw puzzles and put them into one box.

Doyle softened his voice. "You weren't wrong to suspect her. She lied. That tonic bottle was never discarded."

"A classic misdirection, wouldn't you agree?" Houdini said. "Which is why we must return to my original theory: they all did it."

"You mean *my* theory," Doyle said. "I was the first to suggest it, if you recall."

"Let us agree that it was the combination of two brilliant minds working together, and we shall say it is *our* theory."

"Sheesh," was all I had to say.

Doyle's eyes gleamed. "Consider it! Four suspects.

Four motives. Four opportunities. A shared intent to be free of Delilah's hold over them."

"But why poison Irene?" I kept my voice low. "If they're all in it together, why would they try to get rid of her?"

"She's the weak link," Houdini said simply. "Talks too much. Typical woman."

I stared at him. "Did you just say that out loud?"

"You must admit she's prone to emotional outbursts. She nearly gave the game away more than once."

"Poisoning her could be a message," Doyle added. "Or a cover. Make her look like a second victim to protect the rest. To protect Rosalie."

I opened my mouth to argue but stopped. That actually made sense. "Irene and Rosalie were the obvious suspects, but since Rosalie wasn't here for the past hour, she's in the clear."

All the pieces might not fit perfectly, but they sort of fit. Were the ghosts right and all of them worked together to get rid of Delilah? I felt like we were trying to force the evidence to fit the theory. Maybe they were right about all the evidence, but wrong about what it meant.

Filling a pitcher with filtered water, I grabbed several glasses and a sleeve of saltines and pushed open the door with my elbow.

Irene sat on the settee, pale but upright, her head resting against Greg's shoulder. The minute she saw the crackers, she perked up.

"I thought you might want something bland." I

handed her the saltines. "In case your stomach was a bit unsettled."

"Bless you," she murmured, plucking a cracker and nibbling at the corner. "I'm sorry to cause such a scene."

The front door creaked open, and a gust of cool, salt-scented air rushed in, followed by Rosalie.

"I drove to where the road crew is working," she said breathlessly. "They said it's going to be another hour or so." She took in the sight of Irene slumped next to Greg. "Are you okay?"

Todd crossed the room, meeting her halfway. "She collapsed."

"It's nothing," Irene protested weakly. "I get low blood sugar sometimes. I was feeling a little woozy, and then I guess I passed out."

Rosalie stared at her for several long moments. "Just like Delilah."

"Delilah had low blood pressure, too?" Irene asked.

Rosalie hurried to her side and squeezed onto the sofa next to her. "I shouldn't have left. Maybe whoever poisoned Delilah came back to finish the job."

Or maybe they never left.

As I poured water into the glasses, I had a few moments to look around the room. Todd couldn't take his eyes off Irene, but was it concern for her health or was he worried that she'd say something to reveal his guilt? Greg seemed happy with Irene leaning on him, but did he really care about her? Irene nibbled another saltine like a woman recovering from a stomach bug.

And Rosalie… well, Rosalie had the air of someone who had been cleared of all wrongdoing.

Behind me, I could feel Doyle and Houdini watching from the doorway like spectral sports commentators.

"We were right," Doyle said.

"Yes, it's clear we were." Houdini reached out his hand, which Doyle shook.

"We make quite a team." Doyle stroked his thick mustache. "Perhaps we should go into business. The 'Doyle and Houdini Consulting Detective Agency.'"

Houdini's smile vanished. "You mean 'Houdini and Doyle,' of course."

"Alphabetically, Doyle is first."

I left the two of them arguing and returned to the kitchen.

If the four surviving board members of the *Holmes Society of Northern California* had conspired together to kill Delilah Smith, they were likely going to get away with it.

I almost didn't care anymore, except for one little detail.

One of them had tried to poison me.

CHAPTER 32

The sun filtered through the curtains catching dust motes in the air as Irma and Jennifer joined me in the kitchen. I stared at my phone, ignoring the teakettle that boiled furiously.

"Are you obsessed with that game again?" Irma asked. "We might need an intervention."

I pretended not to hear her as Jennifer scooped loose tea into the infuser, then poured the steaming water into the teapot.

"More tea?" Irma shook her head. "Never mind the game. We'll have to send you to tea gluttons anonymous. Oh! You could be a tea-totaller!"

Jennifer asked Irma, "Does that mean you don't want a cup?"

"Nah, when in Rome."

"What does Rome have to do with it?" Jennifer asked.

"It's just a phrase," Irma groused. "Don't they teach young people anything these days?"

Jennifer set out three teacups and filled them to the brim while I continued my research.

Irma took her cup and poured the contents into a mug. "What?" she said in response to Jennifer's raised eyebrows. "I like a mug better. Hey, April."

"Huh?" I looked up from my phone.

"You haven't said much about your ghost buddies lately. Are they still hanging around?"

"Doyle and Houdini?" I asked, as if I currently had any other ghostly friends. "Yeah, and they have an interesting theory."

Irma raised one skeptical brow. "Do tell."

"They think all of them plotted it together. That the whole bunch—Rosalie, Irene, Todd, and Greg are all responsible for Delilah's death."

Irma let out a low whistle. "They must have turned against Irene. Afraid she'd blab, probably. She's lucky she didn't drink more of that tea."

"Was that luck?" I asked, meeting her eyes. "Or was that part of the plan?"

The low battery indicator on my phone was flashing red, but I was so close to the truth I couldn't stop yet. I found the information I'd been searching for just as the lights flickered on in the kitchen and the refrigerator began humming.

"Yay!" Jennifer called out, joining with cheers coming from the other room.

Relieved that we had power again just when I needed it, I turned to Jennifer. "Can I borrow your printer?"

"Sure. It's in my room."

Before she could ask me what I needed it for, I hurried up the stairs. It took me several minutes before I figured out how to pair the printer to my phone, but I finally got the printouts I wanted and headed back downstairs.

Back in the kitchen, I plugged my phone in. Moments later, it buzzed, and I glanced at the screen.

Irma noticed my smile. "What's that about? You're grinning like the cat that got into the cream."

"The sheriff's alert system says there's been a delay, and the road won't be open for at least another two hours." I set the phone back down.

"So why are you smiling?" she pressed. "We're stuck with them for two more long hours. I hope you understand my sacrifice for staying here to protect both of you when I could be at home watching *Touched by an Angel* reruns."

"Yeah, it's going to be a long two hours, but the thought of having them all out of my house makes my heart glad." I couldn't wait for it all to be over. "It's like trying to host a tea party inside a pressure cooker."

Irma nodded. "No kidding. So back to the murder. You think your ghosty friends are right? That they plotted together to get rid of the old bag?"

"Nope."

"What do you mean, 'nope'?"

"You'll find out shortly." I took a deep breath to brace myself and pushed the kitchen door open. "Wish me luck."

"No!" Jennifer called out after me. "You never say good luck. You say break a leg."

I smiled and made a silent wish that I'd survive the next several minutes with no damage or broken bones.

Irma and Jennifer followed me into the front room and stood against the wall like a couple of bouncers. Greg and Irene slumped on the sofa while Rosalie stood looking out the window. Todd sat in a wingback chair with his long legs stretched out before him, scrolling through his phone. He didn't look up.

"You saw the alert?" I asked.

He scowled. "Two more hours."

"Two more hours," Irene repeated. "I can't take much more."

The energy in the room hung heavy and stale. I stood near the hearth and drew a breath.

"Let's talk about Delilah."

Eyes lifted, faces turned. Rosalie's hand tightened around the arm of the settee while Irene, sitting next to her, looked bored. Greg shifted in his chair, uneasy.

"I know she wasn't exactly your favorite person. In fact, you all hated her. But for some reason, you kept working with her. She had some kind of hold over each of you. Otherwise, why stay?"

They didn't answer.

"I know Delilah didn't die of a heart attack. Or stroke. Or any natural cause." I let that sink in. "She was poisoned."

CHAPTER 33

Rosalie frowned. "We already know what you think, and we don't care."

"What you might not know, is that the poison she drank didn't come from the tonic Rosalie brewed, though she admitted it contained trace amounts of gelsemium. Maybe that's what gave the killer the idea. But Delilah never drank the tonic, even though Irene said she did."

"I *did* give her some," Irene insisted. "I had no idea there was poison in it."

With a withering stare aimed at her, I continued, my tone calm but firm. "The poison that killed Delilah wasn't in the tonic. It was in her teacup."

I had everyone's full attention now. Todd straightened in his seat.

"And one of you took that cup away," I continued. "Switched it with a clean one just in case someone decided to test it later for toxins. Most likely, the switch happened as the event was ending. Delilah asked me if she could lie down somewhere. She said, and I remember her words exactly, 'I feel woozy.'"

I turned my eyes to Irene. Greg and Todd did the same.

Rosalie blinked. "Why does that matter?"

"Because," Todd said slowly, "Irene used the same words right before she collapsed."

"What are you suggesting?" Irene asked gaily as if she were amused.

"I'm suggesting that it wasn't Greg or Todd that put the poison in your teacup. You added it yourself."

"You think I poisoned myself?" She forced a laugh. "That is completely ridiculous. Why would I ever do that?"

"Because your attempt to poison me failed," I said. "When Irma spilled my tea, with its fatal dose of gelsemium, and took the cup into the other room, you panicked. You worried we were onto you, so you gave yourself a small dose. Then added more poison to what was left in your cup. If it were tested later, it would back up your story."

Irene's mouth opened, then closed again.

Greg snorted. "That's ridiculous. She would never do something like that."

"You almost had me there, Irene," I continued. "You only made one mistake. Well, two if you count repeating Delilah's words. But your real mistake? You recovered too quickly."

Todd tilted his head. "What do you mean?"

"Sir Arthur Conan Doyle wrote in his paper that the recovery period for a non-fatal dose of gelsemium is several hours. And yet…" I gestured to Irene, who looked alert, even defiant. "An hour later, you seem quite perky."

"I have a very healthy immune system."

I ignored her remark. "At first, you were fine letting me think Rosalie poisoned Delilah. Did you know, Rosalie, that your friend tried to frame you for murder?"

Rosalie grim expression told me she knew what I was saying was true.

"And then, when that didn't stick, you were perfectly happy letting me think it was Greg. Or Todd. After all, when your tea was poisoned, Rosalie wasn't even here."

Greg sat forward. "She wouldn't do that to me. She said she…" His voice trailed off. "She cared about me."

"If that's true," which I doubted, "Then she would have found a way to pin it on Todd. None of you would miss him much, would you?"

Rosalie stood abruptly and walked over to where Todd sat and took his hand in hers. "I would have."

Greg stared. "But… why? I mean, yes, none of us are sad that she's gone, but murder? Why would she do such a thing?"

"Irene?" I figured I might as well give her a chance to explain, but her only answer was a glare. "No? Okay, let me see if I've got it right. I kept thinking about what Delilah said to you yesterday during the event."

Jennifer spoke up for the first time since we'd entered the room. "That's right. Delilah told Irene, 'If you don't tell him, I will.'"

"If you don't tell him..." Todd repeated, brow furrowed. "Tell who? And tell them what?"

My phone buzzed. I glanced at the screen and answered the text with a thumb's up emoji.

"I've been doing some research," I said carefully, watching Irene's face. "The internet is a marvelous thing. Watch a few videos, and you can learn how to disappear without a trace. Or, if you'd rather, you can reinvent yourself and create an entirely new identity."

"Nothing new about that," Irma said. "All you need is a social security number and you're good to go."

"True. But it's harder to keep secrets these days. If you know how, you can find out someone's true identity after they've done their best to leave their old life behind. Ever notice how camera-shy Irene is?"

Todd nodded slowly and turned to Irene. "Now that you mention it, yeah. At every event, you'd disappear when I started taking pictures. And it's funny, but Delilah always made excuses for you."

"I'm just not photogenic." Irene's voice had gone tight. "Some people don't like having candid pictures taken, Todd. I would have been happy to sit for you if there was good lighting and I was able to have my hair and makeup done."

"But despite Irene's efforts to dodge the camera, I did find this." I pulled a printout from my pocket and unfolded Irene's picture, holding it up for everyone to see. "Among all the pictures on the society's website, this is the only one I could find of her."

"See," Rosalie said, "you look nice in that picture. I

don't know where you got the idea that you're not photogenic."

"I agree," I said. "But that's not the real reason why Irene avoided having her picture taken. You see, if you have a photo of someone, you can do a reverse image search."

Greg looked confused. "A what?"

"You upload a photo, and it finds websites where the same image is posted. It can also find similar images, which is what I found."

Irene gave a bored sigh. "This is very interesting, but I think I've heard enough. Let's go, Greg."

Greg's eyes widened. "I'm not going anywhere. Not until I find out what April is getting at." He turned back to me. "What *are* you getting at?"

"The reverse image search brought up this picture." I pulled another printout from my pocket and unfolded it. The second image showed a younger woman with the same sharp cheekbones and tilted eyes. The resemblance was undeniable.

Greg gave me a puzzled look. "So, you found an old picture of Irene. What does that prove?"

"This isn't a picture of Irene." I handed him the image so he could get a closer look.

Greg's brows drew together as he stared at it. "Then who is it?"

"Marlaine Louise Brooks."

Irene's face turned to stone.

CHAPTER 34

The silence was deafening. Irene went completely still, like a deer caught in headlights.

Irene, or rather Marlaine, walked over to Greg, her chin held high like an actress refusing to break character after the director had called "cut."

"That's not me," she insisted, her voice sharp. "It doesn't even look like me."

Rosalie snatched the picture from Greg and stared at it for several seconds. "Yes, it does. It looks exactly like you."

She handed the picture to Todd who asked, "Who is Marlaine Louise Brooks?"

I took a deep breath and began to tell them what I'd learned. "Marlaine is a woman who wanted to escape her past, and who could blame her? When she was twenty years old, Marlaine was convicted of manslaughter for killing her boyfriend. She served seven years of a ten-year sentence."

Rosalie's hand flew to her mouth. Jennifer gasped softly beside me. Irma, arms folded, gave a low whistle and muttered, "Didn't see that coming."

Greg stared at Irene, his voice barely a whisper. "Tell me this isn't true."

Irene stroked his arm as if consoling a child. "You believe her over me?"

Slowly and deliberately, he asked again, "Is this you?"

"Greg, I—" Her voice faltered. "It was a long time ago. I was trying to put it all behind me. You don't know the whole story. It was self-defense, but the lawyer said that the jury would never believe it. They talked me into a plea bargain. I had to say I was guilty, but it wasn't my fault."

He pulled his arm away from her. "You lied to me. To all of us."

Irene's carefully constructed composure began cracking like ice in spring. "Delilah is the one who lied to you. She invented a new name and a new identity for me. And when she introduced me to all of you, for the first time I had friends." She turned to Greg. "I had love. I had you."

Greg shook his head. "I can't believe it."

"It's not what you think. I was young, I was scared."

"You killed someone," Todd said flatly.

"I served my time." Tears began to roll down her cheeks. "Seven years of my life. I paid for what I did. Why should I have to keep paying?"

Greg stood up abruptly, backing away from her. "Was everything a lie?"

"Of course not." She took a step closer to him as if trying to bridge the gap between them. "My feelings for you are real, Greg. Everything between us is real."

"Everything?" His voice broke. "You told me your parents died in a car accident. You told me you grew up in Oregon. You told me you'd never been in love before."

Irene wiped her eyes with the back of her hand, smearing her mascara. "My love for you is true."

"You're pathetic."

The words hit her like a physical blow. Her face crumpled, then twisted with rage and her manner changed from regret to fury. Her eyes locked onto mine, burning with anger. "You ruined everything," she hissed. "I wish you had drunk the poison. I wish I had enough for all of you!"

Her words hung in the air, thick and buzzing like a hornet's nest.

Rosalie gasped. "You tried to kill April?"

"She couldn't leave well enough alone!" Irene's eyes blazed as she looked at me. "We were all happy with Delilah gone. All of us! You should have just let it be."

She began backing toward the door, her voice rising with each step. "Yes, I got rid of Delilah! And none of you were sorry she was gone. I saw how hard you all tried to act like grieving friends." Her eyes flicked to Greg. "I would've made you a good wife."

Greg refused to look at her, staring at his hands instead.

Todd moved to block her path. "Where do you think you're going?"

"The road's about to open. I can disappear again. I did it once, I can do it twice." She reached into her pocket and pulled out a set of keys which she jangled defiantly. "I'll be taking your precious BMW, Greg."

Irma appeared next to me. "You're not going anywhere."

"Watch me." Irene lunged toward the door, but Rosalie was faster. She stood by Todd, the two of them standing between Irene and the front door.

"Irene, don't," Rosalie begged. "Stay and let's figure this out."

"Get out of my way!" Irene shoved Rosalie aside, sending her stumbling into Todd who managed to keep her from falling.

"You won't get away with this." Rosalie made it sound like a threat.

"Oh, no?" She laughed. "Just watch me. Ta ta, losers."

With a dramatic flourish, she flung open the front door and took off in a run.

"April!" Jennifer cried. "She's going to get away!"

"No, she's not." I said calmly, though my heart thudded like a bass drum.

Almost before the words left my mouth, Irene reappeared in the doorway, her arm firmly held by none other than Sheriff Andrew Fontana. His expression was cool, composed, and very manly. Of course, I was biased considering he was my boyfriend.

"That couldn't have been planned any better," he said with that slight, boyish smirk of his.

Behind him my favorite coroner, Dr. Freddie

Severs, entered. When she spotted me, she gave me a nod. Taking up the rear were two uniformed deputies.

Irene squirmed, her fingers clawing at Andy's sleeve. "Let go of me! You're making a big mistake! I haven't done anything wrong!"

"Save it for the judge," he replied smoothly.

One of the officers stepped forward and slapped the cuffs on her wrists and led her out the door.

"Wait, how did you get through?" Irma asked, blinking as if the cavalry had materialized from thin air. "The road's not open yet."

"Officially, it's not," Andrew said. "Not unless you happen to be emergency personnel."

Freddie grinned. "We managed to keep that information to ourselves. The sheriff even got the deputies that run the alert system to adjust the estimate that got sent out. Well done, April."

I allowed myself one deep, satisfying breath.

Jennifer hurried to my side and gave my arm a squeeze. Irma nodded approvingly. Rosalie slumped in her chair, as if her bones had finally given up trying to hold all that stress together.

I gave Andy my warmest smile. "You really do have impeccable timing."

He winked. "I aim to please."

CHAPTER 35

My heart fluttered at Andy's playful comment. "Would it be unprofessional of me to give you a hug? I could really use one."

Instead of answering, he folded me into his strong arms, and I lay my head on his chest. The rhythmic beating of his heart and the warmth of his embrace soothed me into a level of calm I didn't think was possible considering the events of the past two days.

After reluctantly stepping back, I led Freddie upstairs to the parlor where Delilah's body lay in the dim parlor. The thick velvet curtains filtered the light, giving the space a hushed, chapel-like quality. I let the door fall shut behind Freddie and returned to the main floor.

After Todd, Rosalie, and Greg gave their statements, they came into the kitchen to say goodbye. Todd and Rosalie were holding hands, and I hoped if nothing else, that they would stay friends.

"You okay?" I asked Greg. I knew he'd had feelings

for Irene, and her betrayal would take some time to heal from.

"I think so." His voice was hoarse. "Thanks. For everything. For putting up with us. For figuring out who poisoned Delilah. I just wish it had turned out to be someone else. Like a complete stranger."

"I get it. You know, most people get fooled by someone they trust at least once in their lives," I said gently. "Some of us just get there in more dramatic fashion."

He gave a tight chuckle. "Delilah had this way of making you think she was your last chance. And once she had you believing that, you'd do anything not to lose her. Even if it meant putting up with things you shouldn't."

I nodded. I didn't need to say anything else. The man had been through enough.

Just then, the sound of slow, purposeful footsteps descended the back stairs. Freddie appeared, looking like she'd just walked through a fog of serious thought.

"I'll wait here until they come to collect her body," she said. "Based on my preliminary examination, I'm confident the toxicology report will confirm poisoning."

Andy entered the room, and I asked him and Freddie, "Would you like a cup of tea? I can make a pot."

"Tea?" Irma sprang from her stool nearly knocking it over. "Don't you think we've had enough tea? I think we've earned something stronger, don't you?"

"Like one of Jennifer's triple espressos?" Andy asked.

"Don't be cheeky, Sheriff. I mean champagne. It's time we toast to the living."

"I'm still on the clock," Freddie said.

Andy grinned. "That's too bad, Dr. Severs. I'm off duty, but you enjoy your tea."

Irma knew just where to find the good champagne, and we all headed for the front room where we could get comfortable.

Andy guided me over to the settee, even remembering what it was called, and patted the spot beside him. I sat, grateful to let the last twenty-four hours melt away.

Irma popped the cork and poured generous flutes of bubbly which she passed around. She raised her glass. "To justice."

"To justice," we echoed, and I added, "and to friends who know how to spill the tea, literally and figuratively."

"I almost forgot to give Freddie the teacup to get tested." I started to get up, but Andy held out hand to gently stop me.

"What teacup?" he asked. "And why are you having it tested?"

He wasn't going to like what I was about to tell him, but I figured I might as well get it over with. "We're pretty sure Irene, or whatever her name is, put poison in my tea. Irma knocked it out of my hand before I could drink it."

Andy nearly dropped his champagne flute. "You *what?*"

Freddie paled. "Are you serious?"

"I didn't drink any of it," I assured them. "No harm no foul, right?"

Irma spoke up. "No one was getting poisoned on my watch. Well, except Delilah, but that doesn't count."

"What made you think someone had put poison in my cup?" I asked.

"I didn't like the way that woman kept eyeing April. That was a 'one lump or two' kind of glance. And I don't mean sugar. And then when I saw her sitting in this room alone with everyone's teacups on the table, I just knew something was going on."

Freddie blinked. "You saved April's life."

Irma shrugged. "Wouldn't be the first time."

That earned a chuckle from everyone except Andy.

"I'm taking the rest of the week off," Irma announced. "For recovery."

"You deserve it," I said.

"We *all* do," Jennifer chimed in. "Good thing the tearoom is closed tomorrow."

"The tearoom is closed until further notice," I added.

Jennifer tilted her head. "If I know April, that means until Wednesday."

"Exactly." I winked. "Although, we don't have many reservations for Wednesday or Thursday, and considering we've just had a major earthquake..."

"Not to mention all the landslides and road closures," Andy reminded me.

"Yeah, that too. Let's not open until at least Saturday."

"Yay!" Jennifer clapped her hands. "A mini vacation.

I've been wanting to see the costume exhibit at the museum. What are you going to do, April?"

I looked at Andy, who got the message.

"I'm about due for some time off," he said. "I'll be needed for at least the next day or two, but if I can arrange it, how would you feel about a long drive up the coast Thursday or Friday?"

"Perfect." That gave me a few days to lie around the house, watch TV, and see if I could figure out how to get rid of my ghosts.

As if on cue, they appeared in front of us, Houdini eyeing the newcomers and Doyle looking proud of himself.

"We're back," Doyle said. "And this time I'm absolutely confident that we have solved the murder."

"Great," I said. "You can tell me all about it later. Right now, I'm busy."

Doyle's confused expression matched Andy's. I had a feeling Freddie knew exactly what was going on.

"New ghosts?" she asked. "Or is someone making a return appearance?"

"Oh, they're new. New to me, that is."

Andy nodded, only starting to get used to the idea that I saw and talked to ghosts.

Jennifer could hardly contain her excitement. "Tell him who they are." She turned to Andy. "You're never going to believe it. Wait until you hear."

Freddie laughed. "The suspense is killing me."

"Andy, Freddie, meet Sir Arthur Conan Doyle and Harry Houdini."

Freddie gasped and Andy gave me a look of astonishment. No one said a thing for several long moments.

"Well, don't that beat all," Andy said shaking his head. "You must run a very exclusive establishment based on the quality of your ghostly guests."

Irma spoke before I could. "People are just dying to get in."

Jennifer grinned. "What I hate is when they make a reservation and then ghost us."

I didn't know whether to groan or laugh. "At least they don't eat much, unlike our last guests."

The laughter faded as if we'd all suddenly remembered that a woman had died under this roof. No matter what sort of person she was, she didn't deserve to be murdered.

A hush came over the room, the kind that often comes at the end of a very long story.

CHAPTER 36

The following morning, the tearoom felt unnaturally quiet as I carried my cappuccino into the front room. When I'd first moved in, I thought I'd spend half my time sitting by the window or on the porch watching the waves break, but even the best things in your life became ordinary if you didn't remind yourself how special they were.

Jennifer emerged with a mocha latte for Irma, who leaned back in the sofa with her feet propped up on an ottoman.

"I'm thinking of taking Zoe on a vacation," Irma announced. "Maybe somewhere with no tea. No murder. No eccentric people devoted to dead authors."

"Hey!" Jennifer said as she set the mocha on an end table. "Jane Austen may be dead, but she's one of the best authors ever."

"You know what I mean. The oddball ones who dress up and…" she stopped talking just in time. "Not you. You're not an oddball."

"Some people think I am." Jennifer stared at Irma until I thought one of them might start squirming. "Some people might call *you* eccentric."

Irma grinned. "That's because I *am* eccentric."

"You could go to Kansas," I suggested. "I've heard the percentage of oddballs is very low there."

Irma raised her mug in my direction. "Exactly. I vote for Kansas. Wait. Isn't it flat there? I'm not sure I want to go somewhere flat. I've never been somewhere you can see all the way to the horizon."

I stared at her in disbelief. "Really? You have traveled outside of California, right?"

"Of course I have," she said as the doorbell jingled. "But not the middle part of the country. I don't like to be too far from the ocean. Are you expecting someone?"

We hardly ever got unexpected visitors. I had hoped that Jennifer would get the door, and I wouldn't have to get up, but finally I stood and said, "Only one way to find out."

I crossed to the door and opened it cautiously.

No one.

Just the gentle breeze off the ocean and the familiar cry of gulls arguing over someone's discarded bag of chips.

I looked down.

A small brown package sat on the welcome mat. No postage. No return address. Just my name, *April May*, written in flowing, old-fashioned script. The kind of handwriting that made you think of love letters and curses. I picked it up carefully and closed the door behind me.

Jennifer and Irma were already hovering, curiosity radiating from them like heat from a toaster.

"Ooh. A present?" Jennifer asked.

"Anthrax?" Irma suggested.

I gave her a scowl then turned the box over in my hands. It wasn't ticking. It didn't smell suspicious. I glanced at Irma who shrugged, which was as close to approval as I would get from her, so I opened it.

Inside, nestled in tissue paper, was a single vintage teacup. Pale blue with delicate gold scrollwork around the rim.

"Oh my," I turned it over in my hands, investigating the beautiful floral pattern and vivid colors. "It's stunning."

Jennifer hurried over for a look. "There's a note."

It was tucked in under the saucer. I unfolded it, and the paper crackled in that satisfying way paper always should.

You've got good instincts. Let's see how you handle this one.

No signature.

"What does that mean?" I asked, but no one had an answer.

Jennifer's eyes widened. "Is that a threat?"

Irma leaned in, squinting. "If it is, it's a rather benign one. Maybe it's a test, like to see if you can join the very secret society of amateur sleuths."

I ran my thumb along the rim of the teacup and couldn't help thinking there was something oddly familiar about it. But I couldn't place it. Not yet.

"Well," I said slowly, "I don't think it's a threat. Do you really think there's some sort of secret society for amateur sleuths? I wouldn't mind meeting other people who keep having to solve murders." I smiled. "And anyway, after the weekend we've had, a mystery without a corpse sounds almost relaxing."

I carefully rewrapped the teacup and placed it back in the box.

"You're not going to display it?" Jennifer sounded disappointed.

"Not until I'm sure we're done with the aftershocks. It was bad enough that I lost some of my favorite teacups. I don't want anything to happen to this one until I figure out what that note means."

After placing the box on a shelf, I said, "I think I'll put the kettle on."

Irma groaned.

Jennifer grinned.

And somewhere out there, the ghosts of Sir Arthur Conan Doyle and Harry Houdini were looking for their next case.

THANK you for reading Tea is for Trapped, the tenth Haunted Tearoom Cozy Mystery. To learn about future releases and get special bonus content, sign up for updates at karensuewalker.com.

NOW, read on for recipes!

RECIPES

THE RED-HEADED LEAGUE MOCKTAIL

Serves one

A crimson, fizzing tribute to the cunning minds of Baker Street! This refreshing mocktail combines tart cranberry, zesty lime, and bubbly ginger ale for a drink that's as clever as its name.

INGREDIENTS

- 3 oz cranberry juice (100% juice preferred)
- 1 oz freshly squeezed lime juice
- 4 oz ginger ale
- Ice
- Lime wheel or twist, for garnish
- Fresh cranberries or mint sprig (optional), for garnish

INSTRUCTIONS

- Fill a highball or rocks glass with ice.
- Pour in the cranberry juice and lime juice.
- Top with ginger ale and stir gently.
- Garnish with a lime wheel or twist. Add fresh cranberries or mint if desired.
- Serve immediately and enjoy your clever concoction!

Note: To make several at once, just use the ratio of 3 parts cranberry juice, 1 part lime juice, and 4 parts ginger ale and pour over ice.

MRS. HUDSON'S CLASSIC LEMON DRIZZLE CAKE

Moist, zesty, and topped with a sweet-tart lemon glaze

Makes one 2 lb. (8" x 4") loaf

INGREDIENTS

For the cake:

- ¾ cup (175 g) unsalted butter, softened
- ¾ cup + 2 tablespoons (175 g) caster sugar or granulated sugar
- 3 medium eggs
- 1¾ cups (225 g) cake or all-purpose flour (if using self-raising flour, omit the baking powder)
- 1 Tablespoon baking powder
- 2 tablespoons (30 ml) whole milk
- Zest of 2 large lemons

For the drizzle:

- Juice of 1 large lemon - should be about 10 teaspoons (50ml) or a little more than ¼ cup.
- ⅓ cup (75 g) caster sugar or granulated sugar

PREP

- Take the butter out to soften.
- Zest 2 lemons.
- Squeeze the juice from one lemon.
- Preheat the oven to 350°F (180°C / 160°C fan).
- Grease and line a loaf tin with parchment paper. A round cake pan can also be used.

INSTRUCTIONS

1. Cream the butter and sugar in a large bowl until pale and fluffy.
2. Add the eggs one at a time, beating well after each addition.
3. Mix or sift the flour and baking powder together, then add to the wet ingredients using a spatula or wooden spoon.
4. Add the milk and lemon zest, then stir until the batter is smooth.
5. Spoon the batter into the loaf tin and level.
6. Bake for 40–45 minutes, or until a skewer inserted into the center comes out clean.
7. Before the cake is done, mix the remaining lemon juice with 75 g (⅓ cup) caster sugar to make the drizzle.
8. Remove the cake from the oven, leaving it in the tin

9. While still warm, poke holes all over the top with a skewer or toothpick.
10. Slowly pour the drizzle over the cake, letting it soak in.
11. Cool in the tin, then remove and slice to serve.

NOTES

1. For a round cake, bake about 5 minutes less (35-40 minutes).
2. If using granulated sugar instead of caster sugar, you may wish to pulse it briefly in a blender or food processor to create a finer texture.
3. Store covered at room temperature for up to 3 days or freeze slices for later.

CHOCOQUAKE EARTHQUAKE CAKE

12-16 servings
Prep time: 25 minutes
Bake time: 40 minutes

INGREDIENTS

- 1½ cups (170g) chopped macadamia nuts, pecans, or other nuts
- 1½ cups (120g) shredded coconut (sweetened or unsweetened)
- 1 box chocolate fudge cake mix (or another chocolate flavor)
- Eggs, oil, and water and possibly butter according to the instructions on the cake mix box
- ½ cup (115 g) unsalted butter, melted
- 1 8-ounce (225g) package full-fat cream cheese, room temperature
- 1 ½ to 3 cups (250-375g) powdered sugar
- ¾ to 1 cup (130-175g) semi-sweet chocolate chips.

INSTRUCTIONS

Prep: Remove cream cheese from refrigerator to soften to room temperature. Chop 170g of your chosen nuts (you'll need about 1 ½ cups of chopped nuts).

1. Preheat oven to 350 degrees. Spray a deep 9×13-inch pan (at least 2 ½" deep) with nonstick baking spray. Evenly sprinkle nuts and coconut in the bottom of the pan.
2. In a large bowl, mix the cake according to box instructions with the required ingredients.
3. Spoon the cake batter into the baking dish over the pecans and coconut.
4. Melt the butter in the microwave and let it cool slightly. Using a mixer, beat cream cheese until smooth and lump free. Slowly add the melted butter and beat until smooth. Add the powdered sugar 1/2 cup at a time. Taste after 1 ½ cups and see if it's sweet enough for you. Mix until smooth and sweet to your taste.
5. Dollop the cream cheese mixture by rounded tablespoons randomly over the top of the cake, covering as much of the surface as you can (but it doesn't need to cover it completely). With a table knife, swirl the cream cheese into the cake so that most of the servings will have some cream cheese.
6. Sprinkle the chocolate chips over the top.
7. Bake for 40 minutes or just until the chocolate cake portion is just set. (The toothpick test won't work on this cake).

Notes

1. Earthquake cake won't win any awards for looks, but it tastes yummy! And it's great for a potluck!
2. The cake is done when the chocolate cake batter in the center appears set and springs back slightly when touched—the toothpick test won't work because of the cream cheese.
3. Best served while still warm with or without vanilla ice cream or whipped cream, but also delicious at room temperature.

ROADBLOCK ROCK CAKES

These craggy, golden cakes are rugged little treats perfect for a cozy tea break.

Yield: 12 rock cakes
Prep Time: 15 minutes
Bake Time: 18–20 minutes

INGREDIENTS

- 2 cups (250g) all-purpose flour (if using self-raising flour, omit 1 tsp baking powder)
- 2 tsp baking powder
- ½ tsp ground cinnamon
- ¼ tsp ground nutmeg
- ¼ tsp salt
- ½ cup (100g) cold unsalted butter, cut into cubes
- ⅓ cup (65g) granulated sugar
- ½ cup (80g) mixed dried fruit (e.g. golden raisins, chopped apricots, cranberries)
- ¼ cup (30g) chopped nuts (walnuts, pecans, or hazelnuts work well)
- 1 large egg
- ¼ cup (60ml) milk, plus more if needed
- 1 tsp vanilla extract
- Demerara or coarse sugar, for sprinkling (optional)

INSTRUCTIONS

1. Preheat your oven to 375°F (190°C). Line a baking sheet with parchment paper.
2. In a large bowl, whisk together the flour, baking powder, cinnamon, nutmeg, and salt.
3. Add the butter and use your fingertips (or a pastry cutter) to rub it into the flour mixture until it resembles coarse crumbs—like rough gravel on a dirt road.
4. Stir in the sugar, dried fruit, and chopped nuts.
5. In a small bowl, beat the egg, then mix in the milk and vanilla. Add to the dry mixture and stir until it just comes together. The dough should be stiff but sticky. If it's too dry, add a splash more milk.
6. Use two spoons to dollop rough mounds of dough (about 2 tablespoons each) onto the baking sheet, spaced about 2 inches apart. Don't smooth them—they should look rugged, like little edible roadblocks.
7. Optional: Sprinkle the tops with demerara sugar (or "raw" sugar) for extra crunch, if desired.
8. Bake for 18–20 minutes, until golden brown and firm to the touch.
9. Cool on a wire rack and serve slightly warm or at room temperature.

OPTIONAL ADD-INS FOR FUN TWISTS

- Mini chocolate chips for a sweeter take
- Orange zest for a citrus note
- Crystallized ginger for a spicy kick

For more recipes, sales and freebies, and other bonus content, sign up for updates at karensuewalker.com.

Questions, comments, or feedback? Drop me a line at karen@karensuewalker.com

ABOUT THE AUTHOR

Karen Sue Walker is the author of stories with heart, humor and furry pets including the Haunted Tearoom Cozy Mysteries and the Bridal Shop Cozy Mysteries.

Karen also writes The Last Call Crime Club Humorous Action-Adventure Mysteries featuring Whit, an unemployed stunt double, her grandmother, Bobbie, who wants to be a private investigator, and their rescue dog Kit.

The character of Kit is based on my own rescue dog, a Chi-Poo-Shih (in other words, a mutt).

Download the free prequel novella, *The Last Call Crime Club, How It All Began,* at kcwalkerauthor.com.

Printed in Dunstable, United Kingdom